A JOURNEY THROUGH TIME

BOOK TWO:
THE RABBIT, THE FOX, AND THE MONSTER

A Novel By

C.J HANNUM

Published in the United States of America

Brilliant Books Literary
137 Forest Park Lane Thomasville
North Carolina 27360 USA

ISBN:
Paperback: 979-8-88945-340-6
Ebook: 979-8-88945-341-3

For our four-legged friends,
who are far more than what we see.

I Run, You Chase - C.J Hannum

I see you through the tall grass,
Such a wonderful sight, it could not last,
Just like that, you're long gone,
Far out of my reach,
You run like, the wind blows,
Where you go, only the Gods know,
I'll be here waiting till tomorrow,
With my hidden sorrow.

You may be tall, I may be small,
I see nothing wrong at all,
How can it be a sin after where we've been,
After all we've seen,
'Cause I run, you chase,
Yes, I run you chase,
No matter where, no matter how far.

Someday they'll know they're incorrect,
Fate brought us close, brought us here,
Just know you won't face it alone,
It may be frightening, so hold tight to me,
Take my paw, let's go,
We'll show them they're wrong,
You know I'm not far behind.

'Cause, you run I chase, yes, I run you chase,
No matter where, no matter how far you go,
You run, I chase, (Yes, you run, I chase)
I don't care what they think,
You run, I chase, I will chase, always,
I will be there, waiting for you,
I promise you, my friend, my other half,
Glance back over your shoulder, glance back over your shoulder,
There I'll be forever.

Contents

Part One:
Unnatural

CHAPTER I:

The Rabbit

Animalia was a massive and beautiful continent that stretched from the Atlantica to the Pawcific. The waters were crystal clear blue, where aquatic life thrived in the depths below. Not a single vessel disturbed the surface; the sea creatures lived without any interference. Coral reefs remained brightly colored, and no single piece of plastic floated in the sea. Above, the skies had only fresh air to breathe, and no toxic chemicals poured from buildings. It was a pure world where primates and humans didn't exist; untouched, untamed, unspoiled, and maybe, a bit unnatural. There were no houses, and deforestation was not a problem. However, a man from another world would come and change everything for our four-legged friends. This man was unlike any average human. Carrying within him a powerful gift called "energy." Energy was a life force that existed between Aurora and her home planet, Prehistoria. Somehow, the "Energy" made it to the animal planet where it'd remain.

For now, there was only peace. At this time, in the woods, a warren of rabbits, lay hidden behind a hedgerow. Deep in a bunny burrow, a mother named Diana tended to her litter of kittens. Diana lay in a nest of grass and her fur, keeping the kittens warm. Eyes moist, she looked at her young. "My beautiful babies, the Gods blessed me with yet another healthy litter."

A member who stood off to the side looked over the seven, noticing one seemed incomplete. "Seems one is missing a front leg, ma'am."

"And your point is?"

"Perhaps it'd be best to end it before it grows too much more."

"Are you deaf?!?" Barked Diana, frowning and pulling her kittens close, including the one he commented on. "There have been plenty of bunnies born with missing limbs. They survived into adulthood. She will be no different, is a fighter, and will be treated as any other."

"Yes, ma'am, as you say. I'll leave you to tend to them and let the warren know of the good news." Leaving her burrow, the male hopped off to share the birth of the seven and that Diana was well. Alone with her young, Diana hummed and nuzzled each one, feeling them move around and latch on to feed.

Among the kittens, a tiny doe huddled next to her seven siblings, her pink nose twitching. She was blind, vulnerable, and unable to see until a few days later. For now, she was a furless little pink thing, wiggling up to latch onto a tit. Once the little doe called Cuniculus was big enough, she and her siblings left the burrow to graze with the adults. Outside, the kittens chased one another, bounding through the tall grass, for it was exciting to explore their great play area. One lagged behind, coming along after the group, being Cuniculus. All was well, but soon they'd learn there was danger in their beautiful land. One kitten wandered off and stood away from the group. The individual ate on a patch of clover, never noticing a shadow fly overhead.

"Eyes to the sky!" shouted a member who was on watch for danger.

"Take cover!" Called another.

Suddenly, a bird from above swooped down. Wings beating and legs stretching out, its taloned feet dug into the tiny kitten that screamed aloud. Scrambling, the kitten was unable to break away and was lifted off the ground, reaching his paws out for assistance. "Mommy!"

"Son!" Diana tried to reach him, but in the mad dash to take cover, she was pushed by the other members of the warren, who fled into the slack run. Sadly, it wasn't the first or the last time a member of the warren succumbed to one of the many who hunted their kind, only enforcing their fear to protect the new kittens.

"We have to help him!" Cuniculus said, seeing her brother get nabbed, and carried far off into the sky.

"I think he'd be far beyond saving." Added another, gazing up with wide eyes.

"Children, come, hurry!" Diana ordered, counting those that passed her by. "One, two, three, four, five, six…" When she noticed one was missing. "Wait, where's number seven?" Cuniculus showed a bit of bravery, standing till Diana picked her up and carried her into the slack run that led down into the warren. Within the safety of the warren, Diana warned them to stay close, to pay attention when outside, to listen, look, and learn, that it would help them survive to live another day. "Dear, if you don't hide, you'll be killed."

"But-"

"No, buts, you will run and hide next time there is danger."

With a sigh, she nodded. "Very well, I shall do as you ask, mother."

While all were asleep that evening, the curious Cuniculus crept around the slumbering rabbits and went up the slack run. There, she exited through the hole, looking at the sky. The moon was bright while the white dots sparkled, giving light to the dark. Before she could venture farther, Diana's voice called. "Darling!" Diana hopped out of the warren, rushing to push her daughter back into the entrance. "Come, it's dangerous out here."

"But mother, nothing bad happened. Besides, I wanted to see what it looked like once Solis set."

"No more, Cuniculus. It's time for sleep." Diana returned Cuniculus to her burrow, nuzzled Cuniculus, lying by her. "How about I tell you a story, the Creation Story? It'll help you sleep." Cuniculus leaned close to Diana, listening to the old fable that went back ages, before time itself.

Long, long ago, celestials known as the Great Mother Solis and Father Luna looked down upon the desolate earth. With erupting volcanos, flowing lava rivers, and dark skies of smoke, it was a harsh environment. One day Mother Solis and Father Luna had an idea, a plan for Animalia. They used their powers to make the land livable for life, growing plants and creating flowing rivers. Once the planet was set, Solis gave birth to the first animals: prey.

The prey enjoyed their peaceful lives, eating the greenest grass and drinking the freshest water. The land was new, and food was plentiful, provided by the Gods, to whom they were grateful to. Yet, with how the prey animal's bodies were designed, it took too long to turn back to the earth. Thus, Solis gave birth to new animals: predators. To the predators, she gave one strict order: to eat only the deceased.

Like every fable, there was a villain and a hero. The hero was the prey, while the villain was a fox who betrayed Mother Solis' command and carried out acts of violence against the prey. Solis saw the terrible situation and wanted to strike the fox down on the spot. Nevertheless, killing the fox would make the animals fear her, not love her. Instead, she chose to play by his rules and outwit him at his own game. One day she called all predators together to give them a special gift. She told them that thanks to the fox's senseless killings, their world was going to change drastically. From that moment, all predators would have to hunt for their food. Earlier that day, all prey were given special skills to survive the new changes.

At her last words, the predator's teeth and claws grew long and sharp. Their sense of smell increased significantly along with the desire to hunt, slay, and eat the prey around them. The sight of his bloodthirsty friends caused the fox to panic, fleeing in fear while the Great Mother called after him. "Fox, you will be hated by all other animals for what you've done. Craftiness, slyness, and untrustworthiness will flow through your veins and your pups. Forever it will be known as the Curse of the Cunning."

As the days went by, Cuniculus was several months old, and a few bucks from a neighboring warren hopped in for a visit. The females groomed themselves, trying to impress a possible future mate. Cuniculus saw a handsome buck, noticing he approached her. She smiled and tried to sit up, the buck noticing her missing leg, and his face fell, obviously not expecting that. Still, he was polite. "Hello there." He spoke.

"Hi, I'm Cuniculus. Who might you be?"

"The name's Bill. Nice to meet you."

They made small talk, but it was clear he didn't intend for it to go beyond acquaintance. When he excused himself, Cuniculus saw him go to speak with one of her sisters, trying harder with her than herself. By afternoon, all found a match, talking and sharing their stories with the rest.

"Bill says he wants to see me again, can you believe it?" The doe said, flushing slightly.

Diana smiled, yet worried when she noticed not all were percent. "Where's your sister?"

"Which one?" To which several chuckled.

Batting him lightly, Diana gave him a stern look. "Cuniculus, why isn't she here?"

"I thought she came in with us," said Frank, one of Cuniculus' brothers.

"She might be in trouble!" Diana panicked, pushing them to find Cuniculus. When Diana exited the warren, she found Cuniculus, who sat in a clearing. The closer Diana got she heard sniffing, her expression softening. "Cuniculus, it's time to hit the burrow."

"There might still be a buck who's late." Cuniculus turned to Diana, eyes glassy.

"Maybe tomorrow."

"They don't want me." Glancing at her missing leg, she continued. "They'll never want someone like me."

All Diana could do was comfort Cuniculus, who grew a bit hard after that. Indeed, life would not be easy for Cuniculus. She stood less of a chase, being viewed as a weaker member of the group, and she'd constantly be seen as an easy meal. If she were to survive, she'd have to be smarter than the predators who'd hunt her and use her mind instead of her body.

CHAPTER II:

The Fox

Away from the warren of rabbits, elsewhere in the great woods, a fox den was dug below a collection of rocks. Within the den, a mother vixen licked off one of her three pups. Her tail lay over them, like a blanket to keep the pups nice and cozy. The one she was washing turned his head and looked up, unable to make out his mother's kind face. His brown fur was smoothed back, his sky-blue eyes wide with wonder, standing out against his fur color. Snuggling against his siblings, he settled up to nurse.

Her mate stood by, gazing down with a tender smile and the look of a proud father, eyes sparkling with joy. "They are beautiful, my love."

"Indeed, they are." She felt him nuzzle her, licking his snout tenderly.

The three cubs remained in the den till they were old enough to venture out into their territory. The fox pup spent his days with his siblings, playing and leaping about the tall grass. They'd stay low and pounce on the unsuspecting sibling. Doing this would help the pups grow and become great hunters. Rolling along the earth, they playfully bit each other, yipping and enjoying their fun under the warmth of Solis.

"Hey, not fair. You two always gang up on me." Said the larger of the three.

"That's because you make such a fuss, Reed." Teased the only female.

"Now, now, play nice, Vulpes, Eve." Vivian who remained behind while their father, Ted, went out to hunt. At least one parent stayed behind. Today, it was her turn. "Come, it is time for your nap."

Down the den she went, the three following her, Vulpes shoving Reed to the side. Pawing, Eve shoved them in, going in last. Once they were settled, Vivian told them about the world around them, explaining their place in the food chain. They learned they were predators, that one day they'd have to kill prey to survive. Two of them were unshaken by the news, but the male with sky-blue eyes was uncertain and hoped he'd be able to please his parents. If he wasn't a good hunter, he'd fail them, not only that but his role in life. All he could do was hope one day he'd have a mate, a litter, to prove he was worthy. That evening, Vulpes saw his siblings sleeping soundly. Despite his best efforts, he tossed and turned, sitting up and sighing.

"Can't sleep?" He saw Vivian was awake.

"Yeah."

"Here, come sit by me." Vulpes went to her, laying down while her tail brought him close. "Now, how about a story?"

"Sure, wha' 'bout the Creation Story? I love that one."

"As do I." She smiled and continued. "Father Luna wanted young too. Ones he could watch by night, which was why most predators were nocturnal."

Similar to the prey's story, the predator's tale was told slightly differently, at least from the middle to the end. The fox obeyed the rule Solis set in place, eating only the dead. However, finding food was where the trouble began. Finding dead bodies that weren't already eaten became more difficult, leaving the fox half starved. He held out for a while till he saw his reflection in the water, notching his ribs began to show.

The decision wasn't easy, but it was either kill or die of hunger. Finally, he resorted to killing no one healthy but a sickly buck. Afterward, he told Father Luna what he'd done, and Father Luna took pity on him. While it might not have been right, nevertheless, there was no other way to survive. Father Luna said the fox could kill and take out only the weaker members of the group; that way, the strong would thrive. Doing as Father Luna asked, the fox took out the ill, old, and weak, leaving the healthy to bear vigorous offspring. Things went well for him and the others he shared his food with, mated pairs who had young, older predators who couldn't get around too well. To them, the fox was a hero, a signal of hope, who led by example.

All went well till a buck became enraged at the fox, especially since he killed his deceased father. Seeking vengeance, the buck lied to Solis, telling her the fox killed healthy animals. The buck went as far as to stage fake killing, using berries for blood, convincing Mother Soils of the senseless murders. Misguided, Mother Soils changed the prey and then the predators, who grew stronger and faster and were built for a new age.

After the major change, Mother Solis observed the new world, noticing something was off. Indeed, it was, for when Solis realized those, she saw dead a day ago grazed and looked well, she knew the buck pulled a trick on her. Thus, she saw it fit to punish him, believing it would be just. When she found the buck, he knew he was in trouble, unable to flee or hide in time.

Ruining the balance of the world was as much the buck's fault as it was the fox's burden. So, the rabbit and his kind were punished forced to have a hundred enemies. However, she allowed him and his kind a chance. The rabbits became smaller, but their sense of hearing became stronger, sensitive to the world around them. Their back legs grew longer and more power to carry their bodies to safety over great distances, an ability they'd heavily rely on. And they would dig great tunnels underground to hide, having to graze in fear.

Vulpes was lulled to sleep, finding his dream held no joy, fearful he'd let his family down. By the time Solis rose, Vulpes was groggily and almost dozed off during Ted's hunting advice. When each went on their own to track, Vulpes found a nice mess of tree roots to hunker down and catch a bit of shut-eye. When he eventually rose, he rushed to return to the den, finding Ted waiting. His brother Reed and Eve were there, both catching a small animal and bringing it back to the den, proving they succeeded.

When Vulpes showed up with nothing, Ted held a worried expression. "Vulpes, where is your catch?"

"I umm, well, I didn't get anything."

Reed laughed. "Loser."

"Vulpes, if you can't catch prey, how will you survive? If one cannot provide for themselves, then one cannot provide for a mate or their pups. Tomorrow, you will join your brother and sister and go out together."

"Okay, Father," Vulpes said, lowering his head with shame.

The next day, things didn't look up for Vulpes, who found he didn't have the guts to nab the small field mouse. Making sure Reed and Eve didn't see, he gestured for the mouse to flee, claiming that the prey had gotten away.

Though over time, Reed suspected Vulpes was lying and called him out on letting food go.

"I swear, he isn't even trying. I bet he's doing this so he doesn't have to work as hard, can be lazy while the rest of us pick up the slack." Reed said, glaring at Vulpes.

"I tried, but the prey eludes me."

"Enough, Vulpes." Ted cut in, holding a worried expression. "Whatever your excuse is, it's not enough. If you don't start contributing, then you'll be forced to leave."

"Fine, then I'll go." Vulpes walked away, his family gasping and surprised by his decision. "I can make it on my own."

Walking away, Vulpes felt his heart race, knowing there was no going back. There'd be no family support, no meals brought to him. Still, he couldn't let them know the truth. He couldn't bear the shame of letting his family down. Alone, he went deeper into the great forest, forging his path.

CHAPTER III:

The Chase

On a hill, hidden well out of sight, was the entrance to a rabbit warren. Down in the dark space of the warren, several spoke, kittens running around and laughing, causing a good deal of noise. This, in tune, woke Cuniculus, who was annoyed to be disturbed from her slumber. With a yawn, she stretched, blinking and brushing the sleep from her eyes. Up for the day, she went and passed several, trying to get through and struggling to do so. When Cuniculus reached the slack run, it was blocked by her siblings, who spoke and paid her little attention. She tried to get through, yet none moved. By this point, she spoke. "Darlings, can you please move your fluffy tails."

This got their attention; her brother gave her a surprised expression. "Jeez, someone woke up on the wrong side of the burrow today."

"You're so grumpy in the morning."

"Well, maybe if it wasn't so noisy, dearie, I could get a good night's rest." She shot back, pushing to get by them. "I'm going to eat. Now let me pass."

"Why don't you use the other run?" Her sister asked.

"Because it's farther away, it's not the direction I want to go. And, oh! I don't have time to explain this!"

"I know why." Added her brother. "Because you'll have to pass, mother."

"I'm going now. Goodbye, my dears."

She managed to finally get by, making her way up the slack run, able to see the light of day at the exit point. From the outside, a pink nose stuck out, sniffing and twitching. After a moment, a set of ears rose, moving and listening to the most minuscule of sounds. When all seemed safe, she hopped out and went down the hillside, dashing into a row of briers. Before she left fully, a voice called after her from within the warren. "Sweety, did you leave yet?" No doubt it was Diana, catching Cuniculus trying to sneak out. Diana was very protective of her remaining kittens, especially Cuniculus. She grazed with her, followed her around, kind of smothered her, though it came from a good place of love. Not only did Diana keep Cuniculus under her whiskers, but she was constantly trying to fix her up with bucks from other warrens.

Freezing where she was, Cuniculus wondered whether she should answer or not. Unable to lie, she spoke. "No, not yet."

"For Solis' sake, be careful and stay well hidden, dear!"

Cringing, she paused and rolled her eyes. Turning to the warren, she yelled back. "I'll be fine, mother. No need to fret. I've done this many times before!"

"Oh, don't I know? One of these days, you might not return. Remember what happened to your brother?"

"Yes, mother. I know to listen, look, and learn of my enemy." Cuniculus shook her head with annoyance, sighing heavily. "I've returned so far and will continue to do so, darling."

"All I'm saying is-"

"Goodbye, mother!" She went quickly into the forest, and Diana's voice faded the deeper she went.

The farther she got from their warren, the more her pent-up energy was released. Not that she didn't love her siblings and growing in-laws, nieces, and nephews, but it was becoming crowded. They were practically on top of each other, but Diana, being the oldest and one in charge, argued they simply expand instead of relocating. There were many things Cuniculus wished to say, yet it'd create hard feelings, so she remained quiet and left on her excursions to get some peace and quiet time.

Slipping along the cover of roots, she reached the middle of the clearing. Her black ears perked up, turning to the sound of a twig snapping in the distance. Quickly turning in that direction, she held her breath and froze in place. Glancing from left to right, she saw nothing, relaxing her muscles. After a brief moment of silence, she went to nibble on a patch of clover, content and calm. Cuniculus sought out the freshest grass, for the ground by the warren wasn't producing the greatest-tasting blades. Given they ate theirs off daily, it was unable to feed the many mouths. The forest plants had more flavor in comparison, and it was worth the danger, making her feel alive. Deep down, she knew she wasn't alone, sensed it. The sound of paws rustling, a husky breath. It was him, for she knew it was no other.

Swoosh!

Out from behind tall grass, a fox jumped toward her with claws drawn, and jaw opened wide. She rolled to the side and saw him land where she was, finding nothing under his paws. For a second, their eyes locked, and a spark was shared between them, knowing what was to follow.

She fled speedily, feeling the wind through her fur. He saw her racing away into the woodland, rolling his shoulders, preparing to peruse her. Trailing behind her, he scampered on the dew-soaked grass before he got his footing. He was bigger but not faster, causing him to pant heavily in the warm air. Legs pushed to their limits, he ran with all his might to catch up.

To tease him, she swerved between shrubs and leaped over down logs, doing anything to prolong him.

She peered back and saw him fly toward her, getting past every obstacle with ease. Normally, she managed to escape and bolt to the safety of her warren, where she and her family hunkered down and waited for him to leave. Course, she was scolded for bringing a predator to their warren and told not to do it again. Oddly enough, he never returned to dig them out. Thus, she continued to graze in the woodland, always knowing he'd be there too.

It was an endless game for them to see who'd be successful in the daily chase. Weird as it was, they waited for one other like clockwork. Day after day, they'd wake and venture out, both knowing the other would be there. Unless it was pouring rain or too deep of snow, they'd show up.

Cuniculus gained ground and put a few feet between them, seeing he was a good distance behind her. With a chuckle, she blew him a raspberry and wasn't paying attention. A jolt to her head stopped her, sending her backward like a bug. Dazed momentarily, she sat up, seeing a wooden front porch. Not knowing what it could be, she studied it with a curious expression. It smelled of new wood compared to the old trees around her, and how it got there puzzled her. Plus, it was shaped differently than the forest, having sharp angles and a smooth surface.

The building was a house, but she'd never seen such a creation, so it was a terrifying sight. A growl pulled her out of her thoughts, and she glanced back to see a flash of red approaching her through the woods at great speed. The fox, she forgot about him for a moment, realizing it'd take longer to go around the structure to get away from him. Not knowing what else to do, she dug frantically under the porch, pushing her small body between the wood and the ground. She shoveled dirt frantically, throwing it behind her body and into a pile. Getting most of her from in the hole, she kept going, planning to fool the fox.

The fox sprang out from behind a hedge row, landing and looking left to the right, then right to the left, seeing no sign of her. Then his gaze fell upon the house, eyeing it up momentarily. "Strange, that wasn't there a few months ago. Wha'ever." He had a deep guttural voice with a hit of an accent. Taping his claws to the ground, he thought she might've given him the slip. He inhaled through his nostrils, making sure she was out of his reach before giving up. To his surprise, she must've been nearby, for her scent filled his nose. Sniffing the trail, he followed it to the porch. "Crickey, the sheila gave me the slip, eh?" Peering down the opening, he grinned and flew forward, digging with determination. "Unlike yer bucks, us male foxes dig great." Moving massive scoops of dirt with his large paws, soon his front half was in the now widened tunnel. "Then again, we're better at most everythin' we do."

On the opposite side of the porch steps, dirt moved aside, and Cuniculus popped out of the freshly opened hole. She brushed the soil from her body and crept silently over to get a better glimpse of him. His upper half was below while his long tail swept side to side, humming wafted out while he labored. Arching a brow, she continued to watch with a confused and amused expression. It was odd to see, for bucks considered digging to be doe's work. Therefore, they never helped build additional burrows or lend a paw when extending the warren. Honestly, other than reproduction purposes, they were rather useless, in her opinion.

She shook her head and knew there were more important things to worry about, he was distracted, and she needed to make her escape. Getting ready to run for it, she caught a flash out of the corner of her eye, for the fox blocked her view from the woods with his body.

"G'day, Sheila!" His voice was cool, not menacing in the least. Almost like that of a friend greeting the other. "Where do ya think yer goin' in such a hurry?"

"Well, umm, I umm…." She fell on her back and tried to crawl away, digging her heels into the earth. Back touching the hard surface of the platform, she turned to the porch, then to the face of the fox, never meeting his eyes, only seeing his sharp teeth. "I-I-I assumed you'd still be digging, d-darling." She cowered into a ball of fluff, huddling against the V-shaped corner.

"Ya know wha' they say when ya assume?" He leaned down to her, holding his suave tone. Getting no answer, he poked her with his snout, making her jump slightly. "Well, I'm waitin' little Sheila. Do ya know wha' they say when ya assume?"

Instinct told her to bolt and hide, yet there was nowhere to go, nowhere to hide. With all the courage she could muster, she spoke. "N-no, certainly not." Peering between her paw to reveal long eyelashes, she curiously blinked a couple of times. "I presume you do, though?"

He placed his muzzle inches away from one of her long ears. "Ya make an anus out of me and ye." Suddenly, he laughed, nudging her with his paw. "I made that one up myself."

"What?" She was taken aback, wondering why he hadn't eaten her yet. "Is this some sort of cruel joke? Are stalling, hoping I'll beg for my life. Which I will not do. I still have some dignity."

"No, I just always wanted to tell that joke."

"If you're going to eat me, dearie, then eat me already."

His laughter died down, and he froze, looking her over while his ears went flat. "We've never been this close before. Usually, ya run away before I can even talk to ya or catch up with ya."

"Quit beating around the bush and eat me already." She shut her eyes and braced herself, never once groveling. "Just make it quick, okay."

"As ya wish."

She felt his breath. His jaw opened wide around her. Waiting for her impending doom, she trembled and expected to feel his sharp teeth pierce her skin. Yet, it never happened, and she heard him move back, shutting his muzzle. Slowly, she opened one eye, seeing his ears were low, face glancing to his feet.

"After all this time, I've got ya." The difference in his voice was not of someone who'd won but rather someone who lost. "I thought it'd feel different."

"Different?"

Sitting on his haunches, his shoulders dropped, and his tail swept slowly behind him. His ears flickered, and he swallowed a few times. "I-I can't do it." He spoke, shutting his eyes. "G-go on, I won't try to grab ya."

"Oh-okay." She stammered, watching and making sure he didn't lunge at her. All he did was sit, face glancing to his side. At that moment, she realized he had no intention of killing her.

CHAPTER IV:

The Creature

Cuniculus seized the opportunity of a lifetime, dashing for the forest in small bounds. Before she reached it, an object flew out and over her body. It was a net that captured her, and the blow caused her to roll a couple of times before coming to a halt in the grass, becoming woozy and stunned. Once her sense came together, she cried out, thinking it was the fox attacking her. It wasn't, being a vine-like thing. Trying to bite it, she found the material too strong to cut. She fought with all her might to break free, entangling herself even more.

"Hold on!" Turning fast, the fox rushed to her side. "I got ya."

"What?" She was shocked and saw he gently pulled it with his teeth, able to loosen it. "Easy with the teeth there." Holding still, she felt he was close to freeing her. Though the question arose, why would he help her? Whatever the answer, it didn't matter at that moment. He was about to remove it all the way when a net flew over him, knocking him to the ground.

"Bloody cuss!" Like her, he tried to wiggle out. "Wha' is this?"

While struggling, she didn't notice a pair of feet standing in front of her, blocking out the light of Solis with his tall figure. Her eyes followed the legs up to see an unusual animal. It wasn't like anything she'd ever seen before in her life, and she could think of only one way to describe it, a monster.

The monster wore a chemical body suit that covered him from head to toe. It was colorful, with gray, red, and black markings, giving him the look of a frightening being. He breathed through a gas mask, and a pair of goggles hid his eyes from view. He leaned down, reaching to pick her up.

"Stay away from me, you, you vile thing!" She batted his hand away with her paw. When her paw made contact with the glove, it felt rubbery and weird, making her drawback with disgust, wiggling her paw to shake the strange sensation. "What kind of skin is that?"

The monster chuckled, raising his hand to pull the net up in mid-air. She stared, wondering how he lifted her without even holding the vine thing. With a gulp, she looked past her feet to see the grass, longing to get back down.

The noise he projected from his mouth sounded odd, unlike anything she'd heard before. He spoke an entirely different language than herself, or any creature for that matter. Caught between curiosity and fear, she simply froze in place.

He went over to the agitated fox, who continued to wrestle with the net. The fox ground the net between his teeth when he realized someone was watching him. He stopped and looked up to see a hand coming at him, eyes wide in shock at the threat heading his way. He did what any predator would do in such a situation. First, he growled, warning the monster to stay back. When that failed, he gave a threatening expression. "Rack off, will ya." Snapping close to the monster's hand caused him to withdraw. The monster checked his hand for teeth marks, flickering his fingers once or twice. Finished with his inspection, he clenched his hand into a fist, pulling the fox up in mid-air. The force stunned the helpless fox, for he was lifted from the back end. "Hey, wha' do ya think yer doin' there, mate?" The blood rushed to his head, feeling dizzy. "Put me down!"

The monster said nothing and walked forward, bringing them with him. The fox saw Cuniculus, her expression matching his wide-eyed one. They were helpless and floated up, being taken by the monster into the unknown. What lay beyond neither could say. All they knew was they were in trouble.

The door opened, and what they saw didn't seem too bad. It smelled clean, but there were many mysterious scents. The objects were unidentified, being several strange shapes and colors. Of course, to the monster, it was a couch, a coffee table, and a lamp that sat on a small stand. The rug was tan, while the walls were blue with white trim along the bottom.

"This is bad, terrible even," said Cuniculus in a hushed tone. "Oh, Solis, I hope he doesn't eat us! I don't want to depart from this world today."

"Luna's light, I hope not. It wasn't on my list of things to do today. Though if he does eat meat, I'm sure he'll go for ya before me, seein' how I'm a predator and yer prey."

"How is this supposed to make me feel better?"

"It's not, but it makes me feel better." He had a smirk on his upside-down face.

Frowning, she lifted her head. "Jerk, what makes you so special?"

"Are ya single?"

With a raised brow, she gave him a confused look. "C-come again?"

"Just tryin' to make conversation. Though it's no surprise yer single-" His comment gained a death glare from her, making him laugh even harder. "Wow, for a small sheila, ya sure give off a dark vibe."

"That was a low blow, even for you, darling."

"Easy there. I meant it was yer attitude."

"I thought you refused to my missing paw. For it wouldn't shock me, you'd be that shallow."

They gasped when the door slammed shut behind them, cutting them off from their old world. Going through the living room, they passed a set of sliding doors, entering a steel square room with two tables and a pair of cages. Shelves with vials sat on the far wall, across from the doors. With test kits and notebooks, it was clear the monster was a scientist, keeping objects to study.

With a snap of his fingers, the cage doors opened, and he released her into the smaller one, shutting her inside. She got to her feet and went to the door, looking out to watch him put the fox into the other cage, sealing him inside.

He walked away, and the doors shut behind him, leaving them alone. The room itself was dreary, with grey-colored walls and a tiled floor. It had no windows, only a few lights overhead. They shinned differently than that of Mother Solis or Father Luna, being artificial in comparison. Sniffing the air, she found it to be stuffy, unlike the freshness she was accustomed to. She was pulled from her daze when she heard the fox hitting his head on the cage door. Surprised the monster didn't come in to stop him from hurting himself made her think he didn't care about their well-being.

"Please stop that racket. You'll only hurt yourself even further by doing that. Though it could help that head of yours to work properly, darling."

"Keep yer comments to yerself, doe. I'm tryin' to concentrate!" Rubbing a paw to his head, he took another shot at it, yelping in pain.

"That's a job even on a regular day for you, isn't it, dearie?"

"Whatever." He backed up to ram it again.

"Unlike you, I think I'll try to dig out. Use my mind instead of whatever it is you're thinking with."

She scratched the cage floor, sides, and ceiling, finding it was too strong to dig through. It wasn't made of wood, being hard and too tough. Knowing there was no way of breaking out, at least none that she could think of, she sighed heavily in defeat.

After a while, the fox sat back on his haunches and panted, exhausted, head throbbing. She rolled her eyes, knowing there wasn't much she could do. So, she sat and thought about her family, wondering if she'd ever see them again. While they annoyed her and had their faults, she hated the idea she'd never see them again.

Mother, what would she think? Probably worry herself to death. Guilt washed over her, regretting not even saying she loved Diana before she left. At that moment, she knew she could do one of three things. One: panic until she has a heart attack. Two: Give up and give in to death, or three: remain calm and hope the monster will let them go.

"Maybe, the monster will release us after a bit. I mean, what would a thing like him want with creatures such as us?" She asked no one in particular, simply speaking out loud.

"Maybe he'll just kill us." Added the unhappy fox, rolling his eyes at her naiveness.

She ignored him, thinking a positive attitude was better than panicking. Pacing back and forth in her cage, she heard the most annoying ticking sound, only adding to her worry. She checked on the fox every so often, seeing him sleep his headache off. With nothing else left to do, she fell asleep. Cuniculus slept fitfully in her cage until a loud yip from the fox woke her, jarring her from a deep slumber. Her ears moved like a pair of satellites, picking up on what was going on. Head shooting up, she found his cage empty and the door wide open. Seeing this, she thought he'd found a way to get out. In a few bounds, she hopped over to her cage door to get a better look, wondering where he could've gotten to. The last thing she expected to see was what her eyes fell upon. The fox was flat out on a table, with a couple of circular objects shined down on him like Solis, lighting up his outstretched form.

The monster placed a sharp stinger into the fox's side, filling some clear items with a red liquid. It was blood, and why he took it perplexed her. Perhaps the fox was right, and the monster intended to keep them, drain their blood and drink it. How horrible to be kept alive only to feed some bloodthirsty creature. Would the same happen to her? Oh, Solis, the very thought made her want to faint. But instead of drinking it, he put a white leaf on it and set it aside.

The monster's face was cast in shadow by the operating light, which lit up the fox's body. He spoke aloud, holding a tiny square box to his mouth, recording his finds. Still, she didn't know what he was saying.

He plucked a piece of fur and placed it in a plastic bag. The items were put on a shelf that had the word 'fox' labeled under them. Returning to a hologram screen, he saw the fox's skeleton and heart rate. All information was taken down on a clipboard, and he placed it on the opposite table.

Once satisfied, he picked the fox up and walked back to the cage. He put the fox inside and shut the door behind him, pulling a bungee cord to keep it closed. Standing, he turned to Cuniculus, who jumped back with fright. He opened her cage door, and she tried to back away from the hand coming straight for her, fingers holding a sharp silver string. Poking her with a needle, he injected her with sleeping medicine. Slowly, she felt tired, and before long, she was out cold, collapsing to her side with a thud.

For a brief moment, she woke up to see a bright light above her, the monster's shadow-hidden face looming over her. She was flat out on a cold surface that was still warm from where the fox lay. When she tried to move, her limbs were unresponsive, not even twitching. Realizing she was impaired, she sighed and passed out again. Darkness consumed her, and she was lost in the abyss of her mind. Then someone spoke to her, trying to pull her back to reality. This voice was but a whisper until-

"Eh, Sheila! Please don't be dead. I know ya can hear me, so wake up! Come on, doe!"

Still, under the effect of the drug, she felt warm and fuzzy. The cold room looked different. It moved ever so slightly, like ripples along the water. Then she saw him, the fox. He was scared, his eyes filled with worry.

"Aww, you missed me. I missed you too, darling." Hearing her unusual remarks, he didn't say too much. She was groggy, staggering a bit on shaky paws. "You were sad to think I died and left you, huh?"

"Hah, ya wish. I missed teasin' ya, that's all." Ears falling back, he turned his head to the side. "I never said anything like that."

"Sure, you did, my long ears were witnesses to it, dearie."

"They heard wrong." Before another word could be spoken, she felt her eyes get heavy and slip back unconscious. "Doe!" She heard him say, falling asleep.

CHAPTER V:

The Captured Life

In the days to come, she and the fox were forced to do strange things. A tangled mess of vines was placed on her head, and she had to find her way out of a maze, reaching the end and being placed back in her cage while the fox was taken to do the same task. Another time, she was set on rubber ground. It moved, and she had to run, confused, for she ran in place, making no headway. All the while, the monster stood by, watching her. He was interested in them, and she thought he'd never let her or the fox go, continuing to put them through terrible tasks.

She lay on her cage floor, ears dropped, eyes downcast. Sighing aloud, she wondered how the fox was holding up, for he hardly spoke and kept to himself. Other than a mutter here and there, he wished to be alone, so she didn't say much to him. However, she'd say her thoughts out loud to fill the silence.

"I miss my family and Warren." She said, at last, feeling her eyes well. "I wonder if they're even looking for me?"

"Doubt it. Everyone is replaceable."

Hitting her paw down, she glared at him. "I'm going to spend the rest of my days here. Stuck with you of all animals."

"Well, ya weren't my first choice either. Weren't even a candidate."

"Why am I not surprised by that fact, darling."

She saw her food, wondering what type of meal the monster left for her this time. Nibbling with a bored expression, she ate one leaf, and after a couple of mouthfuls, was surprised, for it tasted delicious. Her nose twitched, and she consumed the greens with joy, feasting upon it, making loud crunching sounds.

"Nice to know one of us are enjoyin' themselves." The fox lifted his chin from the crook of his paws, raising a brow and gazing up at her. "Luna on the river, yer loud when ya eat. And for the love of fish, stop that moanin'. It's makin' me uncomfortable."

"If you weren't such a downer, you'd try to make the most of this situation. I know I am. This, whatever it's called, is wonderful." Her cheeks stuffed full. "I have never in my life eaten upon something so good."

He stuck his tongue out and shook his head, shuddering at what the disgusting vegetable might taste like. "Blah! Gross. It's weird and horrible. Then again, look who's eatin' it."

"I'll choose to ignore that last part. It's like something from the Lands Beyond. That's what it is, a gift from above. Maybe you should try what he gave you. You, *gasp*, might like it."

Rolling his eyes, he rested his chin back down. "Yeah, right, liked I take advice from ya."

"Starve to death then, but don't whine to me when you're lying on the floor dying."

"Ya'd be the first to dance on my grave."

"I'd dig it for you, at least."

"And be the one to push me in."

"Will you shut up and eat it already? I can hear your stomach from over here."

"Yer hearin' is that good?"

"Yes, it is. Now eat."

He leaned down and sniffed his food, seeing a chunk of raw meat. The fat glistened in the dim light, smelling good. Licking it daintily, he ran his long tongue over it. A shocked yet happy expression came to his face, and he dug in. He hadn't realized how hungry he was, enjoying the flavor.

"Hah! Told you you'd like it."

"I'm pretendin' it's ya." He picked up and bit down strongly on a piece of meat, seeing her ears fall flat against the back of her head. Chuckling with amusement, he tore the meat, his teeth, and paws greasy with juice.

Disturbed by the sound of meat being chewed between his sharp teeth, she pulled her ears down and tried to block out the noise. Sitting, she remembered how he let her go, turning to his cage with a grin.

"Funny you say that because you had the chance to kill me yet didn't."

"I was just feelin' merciful, nothin' to make a big deal out of. Why don't ya get back to yer meal, and I'll try and enjoy the rest of mine." He scooted the bowl to the side, turning his back to her.

"Why me? I thought you hated me, wanted me dead?"

His ears went flat, and he groaned and tilted his head back. "Why does it even matter to ya?"

"Well, it's not like I have anything else to do. Can't run or exercise in such a tight space now, can I, darling?"

"It's either kill or starve, Sheila, wha' do ya expect of me?"

"You're not answering my question. All I want to know is why you didn't kill me?"

"Yer a step ahead of me. Figure it out." He tore another piece off, and the bowl rested between his front paws, licking his paws and cleaning his chops last.

Thinking and glancing around, she spoke up. "You didn't kill me because you didn't want to?" He was silent, burrowing in on himself, dismissing her. "I bet you were only messing with me. Teasing me for your own sick amusement." Her ears drooped, and her gaze lowered, knowing he wouldn't answer her. "Guess you're no different from the other predators out there, are you, dearie?"

"I guess I'm not."

Laying down, she licked her right leg to begin cleaning her fur. "I guess not." She repeated with downcast eyes. After a while, she heard the fox stretch, moving around the tiny space. Her ears flickered before his head turned to her, fur unkempt. It was scruffy, though he hadn't groomed himself yet. Nevertheless, the bags under his eyes didn't help his appearance.

"Wow, you look bad. When I say that, I mean worse than usual, darling."

His eyes squinted, and his upper lip drew back slightly. "I'm goin' to be stuck in here a while with ya, aren't I?"

"There are far worse punishments, I'm sure, dearie."

"Yer voice is punishment enough." He spoke softly, feeling his eyelids begin to close.

"Red-furred fool." Muttered the doe before she yawned out loud.

He remained silent, lying curled in a ball of fur. Satisfied that he didn't give her a comeback, she said nothing more and relaxed. Time passed, and she, too, fell asleep, finding a bit of peace in the madness. The day wore on, and soon the fox awoke from his nap to find

Cuniculus eating again, surprised by how much food she could put away.

"Didn't ya just eat? Luna, how much can one little doe put away?"

"You certainly know how to flatter a girl. I hope you aren't that blunt when talking to other females, darling. As for my eating habits, I have a high metabolism. That's why I must eat so much, not that you know or care."

"Yer right, I don't," said the fox with a smirk. "And for yer information, I'm very popular among the vixens."

"I don't buy that, darling."

"Will you stop callin' me that? It's annoyin'!"

"What else would I call you." Brushing her cheek, she straightened up at the realization. "Come to think of it, I don't even know your name. How come you never asked for my name, dearie?"

"Ya never asked for mine, so I figure it didn't matter."

"You may call me Cuniculus if you care to keep talking to me, that is."

"Which I don't, of course. My name is Vulpes, by the way." The last part was but a whisper. Little did Vulpes know but with her keen hearing, she heard every last word.

She smiled, and her gaze returned to his cage, her mind wandering and thinking about him. For as much as he annoyed her, she was glad to learn his name. Perhaps it was because they were trapped. Maybe it was nice to know he had a name, showing he wasn't some savage beast but an animal like herself. Whatever the case, she wondered if he felt the same with her. Knowing Vulpes, he most likely wouldn't bother to remember it, calling her Sheila for some odd reason.

Time passed, and she hopped into her wheel, enjoying the ability to burn off her pent-up energy. The monster gave it to her, realizing she needed to be able to move. Out of the wheel, she leaped, taking a drink from her waterer. It was kept in a large bottle, and a metal spout had a ball that moved, allowing water to pass through it. Done, she went to eat some hay, twitching her nose into the sweet-smelling tuft.

"I gotta say, this is the most I've eaten in… Well, in forever."

"Wow, too bad I don't care."

"Would it kill you to be a little happy?"

"Yes, it very well could kill me. Then where would ya be?"

"Well, I'd be much more positive without your negative comments. You should try to be happy, dearie, for being glooming isn't going to get you out of here any sooner."

"We're never getting' outta here. I've accepted that."

Ears perking, she faced him with surprise. "So, you're giving up just like that?"

"Yup, just like that." Said Vulpes dryly.

"You can't, mustn't, that's being weak-"

"Stop tellin' me wha' I should do, darn it! I'll die if it pleases me!"

"Then die for all I care, darling. I'm just making conversation. You don't have to get all snitty."

Vulpes blocked her out and lay on his stomach, glancing around his cage. He spotted a tunnel along the back wall and figured it led out somewhere. He'd been in the cage for some time and only now noticed the hole in the wall. Standing, he saw his chance to escape, smiling brightly. He turned to Cuniculus' cage with a smug grin on his face, wanting to bid her farewell.

"Well, Sheila, ya were right."

Turning to him with a confident grin, she spoke. "Now you're making sense."

"It's been real, but I think I found a way out. I'll see ya."

Her cherry tone changed to worry. "Whoa, whoa-wait, where are you going? Are you just going to leave me here?"

"Sorry, cutie, but I'm goin' home, so bye, bye." Vulpes smiled, shooting her a wink.

As he walked out and away, she yelled obscene words at him. "Why you no good scruffy low life!" Yet she stopped her yelling, realizing he wasn't coming back. When he was out of hearing rang, her voice trembled and went soft. "Don't leave me alone, Vulpes."

For a few minutes, she simply stood, seeing his cage was bare. It was scary. For now, she was completely alone. While Vulpes was a pain in her tail, his absence was felt. For there was no one to talk to or who understood what she witnessed and had been through.

CHAPTER VI:

The Fight

Vulpes had turned tail and left her in the terrible place. Trying to get herself together, she went to her wheel. She ran off her anger and fear, grumbling under her breath. What boiled her blood was that she let it get to her. Why should she care if he left? He certainly wasn't someone she should look to for support. She was strong and could handle the monster, right? No matter what she told herself, nothing helped.

"How dare he. And to add further insult, he called me cute, the jerk."

The sound of the wheel turning filled the silent room, along with her talking. Her one-way conversation was interrupted by the sound of someone coming back through the tunnel. She froze and stared into Vulpes' cage, wondering what it could be.

Coming out of the shadow and into the light came Vulpes. "Well, look who's back. Come to gloat in my face about how you're free now?"

"No. It was a trick. I couldn't get out." He kept his gaze on the ground, unable to find the strength to meet her eyes. His fur was ruffled, clearing he tried to break out as he had in the cage the day they arrived.

"I see. Did he use his strange abilities on you?"

"There was some invisible force keepin' me inside. I could see through it, yet couldn't break it. I've never seen anything like it. I thought I was free for a moment."

"I'm sorry to hear that, dearie."

"Can ya just give me some space?"

"Well, excuse me for trying to make you feel better. All I wanted, am trying to do is make this horrible place somewhat tolerable."

"It would be tolerable if ya weren't here!" He gasped, wishing he could take it back. But it was too late.

"I see." That was all she could say. "If that's how you truly feel, then I won't bother you again."

His mouth opened and closed, yet nothing came out. With a nod, she burrowed down, feeling awful. Vulpes was her natural enemy, yet here she was, upset by his words, his silly words. They had gone back and forth before, but this was an actual argument that left her feeling gloomy.

Vulpes lay in his cage and peered over his shoulder when he heard a faint sniffing sound. With perked ears, he realized she was crying because he hurt her. He felt a pit in his stomach, a feeling he'd never experienced before.

Gulping the lump in his throat, he hit his paw on his forehead, feeling like the backside of a mule.

They sat in silence, neither one wanting to talk after their fight, not knowing what to say. The only noise to be heard was their breathing and a faint sound coming from outside the steel door. They stayed like this for a while, not knowing what to do.

Vulpes didn't speak a word and went out to lay in the grass, longing to be free and run around his old home. It hurt even more, to see other animals running free without a care in the world. At least he could go out, unlike Cuniculus, who remained in her cage. There it was again, the guilt, the shame for snapping at her. All she wanted was to be nice and treat him well, despite her being as scared as he was, pushing her fear down to put on a brave face. Paws placed over his face, he sighed heavily, unable to believe how awful he'd been to her.

While Vulpes was outside, Cuniculus spent her time eating, running in her wheel, and thinking of Vulpes. They weren't friends, but they weren't enemies either. They had a mutual understanding and respect for each other, an understanding that wasn't common among hunters and hunted. It was an unspoken bond, something she couldn't find words for. She'd known Vulpes for a good portion of her life since they were young.

✳ ✳ ✳

Cuniculus was warned by Diana, to be leery of predators, especially foxes. Foxes were the most feared among the hundreds that tried to kill them. The hundred was a term used to describe the rabbits' enemies since they were considered weak, timid, and easy to catch. In their tales, legends warned the young to obey their parents, stay close to the warren at all costs, or face death.

The fable of the fox was older than anyone could recall. It told of a smooth-talking fox who lured a rabbit away from the warren, speaking and promising false treats. The rabbit willingly obeyed and followed the fox to his den, only to be killed and eaten.

Cuniculus wondered if the tale were true and if a fox would do such a thing, along with other predators in their stories. She'd see for herself, wanting to leave the safety of the warren to go into the forest and possibly observe such animals. That's where it all started.

When she could go out independently without supervision, she felt a mix of joy and fear, not knowing what lay beyond. There, she got her first glimpse of Vulpes, who was close to her age.

Vulpes was a first-time hunter, traveling with his siblings to find food. Sniffing the ground, a scent caught his attention, leading him away from the pair. Following it, he came across Cuniculus, looking at her like she was the most adorable creature he'd ever seen. All she could do was study him, seeing his long tail sweep behind him.

They stood a foot apart and seemed to be curious about one another. He sniffed while her ears moved, both taking a step closer. They were nearing the other when Vulpes' brother came out of the brush. He ordered Vulpes to nab her, so he gave chase.

She was able to outsmart him, using tree roots to mess him up. Caught in the roots, Vulpes struggled and was unable to get loose. Safe, she stopped only inches away, leaning in to get a better look at him, for she'd never seen a predator up close. His snout was long, and his fur hadn't turned fully red, bringing out his eyes. Those sky-blue eyes, orbs that drew her in.

Their eyes locked, and his brother came and scared her off before she could do anymore. All she could do was wonder if their paths would cross again, and the rest was history, for the two met on several occasions.

After several days, the silence became too much for Vulpes to bear. He tried to get her to talk with a snappy comment, to which she acted busy or pretended to sleep. She heard him cough into his paw, hoping to get her attention. Her back stayed to him, making him work to get her interested.

With a groan, he sat up straight and had to speak up. "Seein' how we might not get out of here, let's try to get to know each other a little bit better, eh?"

"Oh, so you want to talk to me now, do you, dearie?" Licking her paw, her ears flicked his way, yet her face never turned. "Cause the last time we spoke, you told me to bugger off."

Vulpes gave a friendly nod, though he kept a smile on his face. "Yer puttin' words in my mouth. I didn't say that."

"You didn't have to. It was clear by the look in your eyes. They're easy to read, darling."

"Come on, I know how much ya missed hearin' my soothin' silky voice. Consider this a gift, my long-eared friend. Yer playin' hard to get, and I like me a challenge."

"Friends, that's a laugh. And there is no challenge if I won't talk to you."

"Ya just did speak to me."

"Starting now, I won't speak to you."

"Fine, sleep well, Sheila." He looked at her with his lovely eyes, tail sweeping back and forth behind him.

With a sigh, she went to the back of her cage, curling up to sleep.

Ears folded back, she breathed steadily, waking when a loud noise woke her. Like the last time she was disturbed, she went directly to gaze out. She saw the monster running around after something. The door to Vulpes' pen was wide open, showing he escaped, attempting to leave the room. Vulpes ran from one end to the other, desperate to get out, yet the monster was fixed on keeping him.

"Vulpes!" Cuniculus said in surprise.

Vulpes ran and ducked under the table, the monster trying to grab him, only to fall face-first to the floor. With the monster down, Vulpes grabbed the bottom part of the monster's jacket, yanking it over the guy's head. With a smile, Vulpes went and jumped up to try and figure out how to free Cuniculus.

"What are you doing?" She called, watching the monster struggle to stand.

"Tryin' to help ya."

"Are you dumb? Save yourself!"

"Not without ya." He said, clawing the wire, biting, and doing all he could to open the door. Suddenly, he was thrown to the floor, moving and becoming ridged. For Vulpes found himself frozen, unable to move a muscle.

Cuniculus gasped aloud, unable to understand how he was petrified in place. Her eyes studied the monster, seeing his one arm was extended, appearing to use his strange powers to hold Vulpes. Not only that, but she then noticed the cut and broken flesh on the monster's arm. From what she gathered, Vulpes must've attacked, breaking loose and trying to flee. The monster made an odd sound, placing Vulpes back in the cage and shutting the door again. Once within, Vulpes slumped to the floor, breathless and struggling to get himself together. The monster kicked the fence with his foot and left to tend to his wounds.

Part Two:
Forbidden Friends

CHAPTER VII:

Can Predator and Prey Get Along

So much had happened so quickly, and Cuniculus' mind was trying to process it all. She was quiet for a moment, peering down to see if he was hurt. Vulpes was motionless, though she swore she heard him breathing. "You dead, dearie?"

Getting his air back, Vulpes spoke. "No." Sitting on his haunches, he cracked his neck before continuing. "I was so close to gettin' us out."

"Us?" She asked, surprised if anything. "I don't understand why you'd try to help me? I've been rude to you."

"With good reason. I wasn't exactly the kindest bloke." He gave a nod, eyes not lying.

"How did you even get out?"

"I pretended to be dead, waitin' till his guard was down before I bite him. Got a few good marks in him before he captured me again."

Touched that Vulpes was willing to help her, she held a small smile. "That was brave of you, but I've excepted my fate. We'll never get out. You were right. We'll be stuck tucked in here forever, till we die."

"I could think of worse beings to be in here with, my brother bein' one." While the monster got the better of him, Vulpes was stubborn and unwilling to give up so easily. "Ya told me not to give up, now I'm tellin' ya. Keep yer chin up. We're close."

Rolling her eyes, she tilted her head to the side with an amused expression. "Sure, whatever you say."

"Hear me out, Sheila. Don't ya want to leave this place once and for all? Do ya really want to waste away in here? Let that thing toy with us like we were nothing. Torture us for his own sick amusement. Is that wha' ya want?"

"No, I suppose not." She showed interest in his words, knowing if they put their heads together, they might stand a chance to escape. "It does sound nice. But the tunnel was but a trick. What if there are more hoaxes outside of here, Vulpes, dear? The monster is smart, and I doubt he'll let us stroll out on our merry way. Not to mention you just got your tail handed to you by him."

"I know, but we can't just sit here like fools any longer." Vulpes bit the wire, trying to pull it loose. "I'll die tryin' to escape if I have to. Besides, ya shouldn't trick a trickster."

"How do you propose we open it?"

"I've been glancin' around, watchin' the monster open and close our cages. He always moves the black stretchy thing." He looked at Cuniculus' cage while she spoke, but he heard nothing, more interested in her sharp front teeth. "That's it! Sheila, chew through that black thing. I tried to get to mine, but my snout was too thick to fit through the small space. Yer mouth should fit through. Give it a go."

"This better work or I'll have your head for this."

"Just hurry up."

She snorted. "A please would've been nice."

Despite a grumble from him, she stood on the fence and poked her muzzle through the small square holes, sniffing it before chewing the rubber. Her powerful front teeth cut through the strap in a matter of minutes. It snapped, and she leaped back, not wanting to fall face-first to the floor. The door swung back and forth on its hinges, and she glanced down, seeing the floor below her, instead of seeing through the metal fence. She jumped down, and the ground felt cool against her paws, making her shiver.

"Well done, Sheila, well done. Now, mine is a bit different, it's hooked up top."

"I'm not an idiot, Vulpes, I can see it." She made a few small bounds to reach his cage, eyeing up the wired door. Squatting and wiggling her tail, she prepared to leap up, and then, in a single bound, she was atop his cage.

Before she went to work, she peered in, and their noses almost touched if not for the metal. "First, promise you won't eat me. I'm willing to help you out, but there is a price for your freedom."

"I swear on my life." He placed a paw on his chest. "On Mother Solis and Father Luna, I promise. Besides, I was risking my neck to save ya earlier."

"Yeah, yeah, I get it. You appreciate me and need my sharp front teeth." She gnawed through the strap, and it broke. The lower half fell to the ground while the upper part hung loosely on the cage. "Ta-dah! You're free. No need to thank me, darling. Though it would be appreciated."

Vulpes slowly pushed his paw on the door, watching it swing open. His pads on the cold surface felt like ice over a pound. He smiled and looked at her. "Nice job, Sheila. I didn't think you'd do it. Guess you've got more guts than I gave ya credit for."

"You were one to overlook true potential, Vulpes."

He crept all the way out and saw her jump down, landing beside him. With a soft hum, he leaned over and licked between her ears, making her leap back. His tongue hanging half out, pulled in as a smile crept over his amused expression. "Easy Sheila, I was only thankin' ya."

"Y-you're welcome." She quickly brushed her fur down and eyed him up, expecting him to attack her.

When he didn't, her nose twitched slightly, wondering why. "You're not going to hurt me?"

"I made a promise, didn't I?"

"Yes, but I figured you lied and would try to kill me anyway." She gave him a playful grin. "Given you imagined eating me the other day, darling."

"How could I lie to ya? Ya'd probably call my bluff."

"Enough talking. Let's get out of here. I'd like to make it back to my warren before dark." She hopped in small bounds, unaware he watched her.

He strolled up beside her. "Yeah, a cutie like ya out and alone at night won't end well for ya."

"Don't call me cute. It's rude, dearie, have you no manners?"

"Jeez, sorry to offend ya. Even though ya offended me several times."

Cuniculus sighed heavily, shaking her head. "It's always about you. You can't take a joke, acting all hurt and pathetic. Such a kit you are, Vulpes dear."

"As ya can see, I am no pup." He glanced down the length of his body, seeing she only rolled her eyes. "Takes all words from ya, doesn't it?"

"The only word that comes to mind is unimpressed." She gave a wink, seeing his jaw drop. Before he could give her a comeback, she went to the door, listening for movement. "It's clear."

"Right ya go before me, and I'll follow ya."

With a sigh, she took the lead. Through the sliding automatic doors, they went, entering the living room. The monster was nowhere in sight, giving them a bit of relief. Cautiously, she hung back, hopping behind the table, to the chair, and a sofa, hiding from some unseen enemy that might be lurking in the shadow. With good fortune, Vulpes wouldn't comment on such behavior. It was embarrassing enough that he had licked her moments ago.

Vulpes watched her, walking out with less fear. "Hey, it's okay, don't be scared. The monster isn't here."

"I'm not scared. It's a precaution, dearie."

He sighed heavily and spoke in a less cocky tone. "All I'm sayin' is, I can smell if he were here. I know it's not sayin' much, but I won't let him hurt ya." Leaning down, he tried to coax her out from hiding. "So, will ya come on out?"

She stared up from her crouched position, eyes large with a hint of fear. The softness in his eyes assured her he wasn't joking around. With a deep breath, she slowly moved her front paw to exit the hiding spot, yet paused.

"I-I guess. But if I see him, I'm bolting. I don't care if you want to stand your ground, dearie. I have nothing to prove to that monster."

"I understand. Now get on out here."

"Very well."

She crawled out all the way and brushed her paw on the strange grass, which was soft but not green. It was weird, smelling of fake flowers. Vulpes was wandering around, seeing something that got his attention. She looked at the wall in front of them, seeing a small table with a box on top. What made her wonder was the fact it was glowing from within.

"What is that?"

"Don't know, but I'm gonna find out." Vulpes jumped up and placed his paws on the table, peering down into the box. "Hey, check this out." The box had a yellow glow around it, and light flowed out like waves, a soft voice called, beckoning them to come closer. "Do ya hear that?"

"And here I thought it was my overly sensitive hearing picking that up."

She climbed up his back and onto his head, trying to get a better look. He tilted his snout, Cuniculus sliding down between his front paws. There she sat, inspecting them, the wheels turning in her head.

"Do you think these things give the monster his abilities?" She looked to Vulpes, seeing he struggled to come up with a good answer.

"Maybe, but why are they callin' to us? Unless they want us over him."

"Let's touch them and see what happens, shall we, Vulpes dear?"

"All right, wha' can go wrong."

They slowly leaned forward and placed their paws on the gloves, gaining quite a reaction from the objects. The watches flew up from the box and wrapped themselves around the animal's paws. The left fastened itself to Vulpes' paw, while the right attached to Cuniculus' paw. They shut their eyes and felt a jolt run through their bodies while the items on their paws placed a glow around them, securing a lifelong bond with them.

The bond can't easily be broken when the watches find the proper host. They connect not just to the mind but to the very soul. Little did the pair realize the Energy they held in them, a power source from an entirely different place and time altogether, from Prehistoria.

For a moment, they thought they saw a female version of the monster, who reached out and placed her hand on either of them. Her dark hair floated like she was underwater, giving her an angelic feel. Her body became light, merging into them. Images and a glimpse of another world flashed through their minds, going by like a movie on speed.

From outside the house, the widows had light pouring out. Suddenly, a shock wave flew out, spreading far and wide. Every land mammal glanced at the strange glow, holding the expression of someone who witnessed a new and wonderful emotion. It lingered and slowly vanished, fading into the sky above.

CHAPTER VIII:

The Watches

Back at the house, the intense glow melted away, and the pair lay on the floor. What happened to them was shocking, dream-like, and, unfortunately, forgotten quickly. They rose and sniffed over one another before getting to their feet fully, feeling light-headed. Their fur stood on end, and both quickly worked to smooth it back down. Their movements weren't quite so animal-like as before and seemed more human, resting on their back legs and brushing their front paws over their bodies.

"That was weird, wasn't it?" Cuniculus patted the last of her fur down, remaining on her haunches.

"Do ya think it might kill us?" Vulpes' paws worked swiftly, brushing his tail out. "Cause I'm too handsome to die."

"I don't think so. Otherwise, we'd be dead by now, at least, I'd assume."

"Ya know wha' they say when ya assume-"

"Don't even start with that stupid joke, else I'll toss you back in the wretched room." She suddenly noticed the home, seeing it was different than when she first saw it. The objects around her didn't seem as scary as before. The smell wasn't so frightening. Lifting her paw, she rubbed each eye, peering around again. "It's weird. I feel like I'm looking through different eyes."

Vulpes wiped his own eyes, blinking a couple of times. "I-I can see in color! Everything is bright, wow. It's so beautiful." When he saw his form, he laughed before he continued. "Luna above! I'm red!"

He looked at Cuniculus, seeing her for the first time, it seemed. She was tan, with black ears and bright brown eyes. They were sharp, hidden behind long eyelashes. Her pink nose matched her bottom lip, which was lush and full. She was, dare he say it, pretty. More than that, he felt drawn to her, like a moth to light. Something told him to stick with her. He shook his head, feeling foolish for thinking such a thing. They were too different, prey and predator, total opposites.

"I can't wait to see the outer world after this. Let's look for the slack run. Hurry now."

It took a while for them to find it, but Vulpes let his nose lead the way. They walked to the wooden red door and sat in front of it, looking up with curiosity, knowing it was their gateway to freedom.

"All we have to do is figure out how to open it. Looks a bit more complicated than the strap. I'll try and hit it." He nudged his shoulder into it, finding it wouldn't budge. Clawing it a few times, he found the wood too thick to cut through. "Well, that's all I got. Wha' 'bout ya, any ideas?"

"Shouldn't be too hard." She shut her eyes and saw an image through someone else's eyes. A hand like the monster's reached out to turn it, opening the door. Blinking in surprise at the information, she glanced up at the knob. "All we have to do is turn that shiny thing, and it'll open."

Vulpes glanced from her to the knob, shrugging. "Let's try it out. I'll do it, for I doubt ya could even reach it, my pint-sized friend." He stood on his hind legs while his upper half stood on the door, ignoring her glare.

"Just open it already, darling."

He used his front paws to turn the knob, hearing a click before it flew open. There she stood, blinking till her eyes adjusted to the brightness. The sounds of the forest filled Cuniculus' ears, giving her a sense of familiarity. She could only stare in awe, seeing her old world with a new frame of mind. It was lovely, wonderful after being stuck in the small square space for who knew how long. Then it struck her. At least she wasn't alone. She had Vulpes.

"We did it. I can't believe we did it!" Bounding a few times, Vulpes could not contain the sense of freedom. "Out from that terrible place at last!"

"Yeah, we're free, free!" She jumped up and down, scampering out.

Down the set of steps she went, rubbing her paw on the grass and taking a deep breath in. The scent of it was delightful, like being home. A pair of butterflies fluttered by, moving rhythmically with one another. They went by Vulpes, whose eyes were the color of the sky. She'd never noticed how beautiful they looked against his red fur. His stature was tall compared to the short, stocky bucks she'd seen, being strong and lean in all the right areas. There was something else, something she couldn't put her paw on, a familiar sense. Flushing slightly, she turned her gaze outward.

"Vulpes, dear." Unable to think of what to say, she stuttered a bit before becoming silent. She rubbed her paw on the wood, thinking about what to say. "Well, I don't know how to say it. Guess, for once in my life, I'm at a loss for words."

"Wha' do ya say we are mates?"

"What!" Exclaimed Cuniculus, fur rising.

"Yea-Oh! I didn't mean we should do that." Vulpes' fur rose, eyes glancing around quickly, trying to say the right thing. "I mean, not that ya aren't cute."

"Cute" Her eyes were wide, looking him over with a skeptical expression. "Mates, what are you getting at?"

He shook his head, and his fur ruffled slightly, struggling to understand what he meant. "I mean, it means friends. We should be friends."

Settling, she took a breath. "Oh, friends. I, I don't know."

"Why? We spent a good deal of time together." He was fishing in the dark for a reason for them to remain together. It was sweet and funny to see how nervous he was. "We're together now and stuff."

"We fought through most of it, darling." She corrected, yet didn't leave. "I wouldn't go off of that."

"True, but we're not now. Things are different, somehow."

"I think it's best if we go our separate ways. Act like nothing ever happened, and return to our playful chases. It's the right thing to do, right?"

"Sure, wouldn't want to cause trouble." Vulpes gave a small chuckle, hiding his true emotions, though his moist eyes told Cuniculus otherwise. "Goodbye, I guess. I'll probably chase ya tomorrow or somethin'."

"Yeah, have a safe journey home, Vulpes." She saw him turn but paused, taking a breath before he spoke.

"No, I need to say somethin'."

"What?"

"I don't want ya to go." Her heart skipped a beat, nose twitching, wondering what he was about to confess to her. Head high, he took another breath. "I want to stay with y-"

He was unable to finish, being sent flying through the air by an unknown force. Slamming into the door, he slumped down in a heap of pain. He struggled to get up, caught completely unaware.

"Vulpes!" Cried Cuniculus, hopping up the steps to reach him. "Whatever happened?" She froze in her tracks when her ears caught the sound of footsteps. Turning quickly, she found the monster walking from the woods. He brushed by her, boots beating against the porch. He went to Vulpes, sending him clear across the deck with a wave of his arm, a red glow illuminating him. Vulpes yelped and hit the ground, helpless to fight back.

"You worthless fox, how did you two get out!" yelled the monster, Cuniculus understanding him for the first time since they met. Though, the voice coming from him was robotic. "I should have kept you on a tighter leash if I'd known you'd plan to escape again."

Vulpes was held mid-air, fighting to break free, yet was rigid in a sea of red illumination. The monster pulled a collar and leash out of his bag, pinning Vulpes down and getting ready to place the object on him. Fear filled Vulpes' eyes because he had no idea what the monster would do to him.

"You leave him alone!" Cuniculus ran forward, hitting the monster's feet, upending him easily. "Vulpes, run!"

He fell and saw her go to Vulpes, helping him to his feet. Reaching out, he held one of her back legs, making her scream with pain. Vulpes bit his hand, growling and shaking it a few times. He released the rabbit, using the Dark Energy to form a wall in front of them. They were blocked and gasped, Cuniculus cowering close to Vulpes, who growled while his fur bristled.

"There is no escape for you now." The monster's eyes glowed from within his goggles, surrounding his entire body.

Cuniculus turned her head from left to right, unable to find an escaped root. "We're trapped!"

"Not if I can help it," said Vulpes, feeling something deep within a snap.

He spun quickly, and earth shot from the ground, knocking the monster in the head and sending him backward. With him out cold and a wall of rock shielding them, they saw the red light vanish, allowing them to leave. And go they did, fleeing for their lives.

Left on the ground and unconscious from the blow to the head, moments went by, and slowly, the monster woke and moved. With the pair out of sight, he cursed under his breath and brushed the dirt from his clothes. He stood and walked up the steps and into the house, wanting to know how they got loose. Going straight to the steel room, he opened the cage doors. The rubber cords bit through, the pieces laying on the tile. Not only that but when he saw the watches were gone, he gasped aloud.

Holding a recording, he spoke into it. "Evening, the subjects are smart and have escaped. I also see they've stolen my other pair of watches, allowing them to use the Energy within." By the box was a picture of a woman with dark hair and eyes standing by a blonde-headed man. "I'll focus on hunting and getting them back, no matter the cost. If they form a strong bond with the Energy, they could prove to be quite a threat, just like Cora." In a fit of rage, he ran his hands over the top, throwing the box to the floor and breaking the picture. It shattered, and the glass shimmered against the picture, lying there while the monster continued to go around cursing and breaking a few items here and there.

CHAPTER IX:

The Debate

The pair ran for a while, crossing a small creek before feeling safe. Stopping for a breather, they tried to collect themselves. Cuniculus looked back, uncertain if they were followed. Her legs trembled, feeling they'd give out any moment. Glancing to her side, she saw Vulpes was in no better shape, dropping his head down between his front legs. He swallowed a few times from the dryness in his throat, breathing hard and glancing at Cuniculus. Able to breathe normally, she spoke first. "Do you think he's coming for us?"

"I don't think so." Taking another gasp for air, he grinned. "Boy, I feel out of shape."

"No, you were fine, dearie. You were faster than me."

"Yeah, right, ya run as the wind blows. Which was probably why I could never catch ya."

"If I recall, I survived because I outsmarted you."

"How could I have forgotten that."

They stopped, resting on the grass, for they hadn't run in a while. Bodies trembling, they sat, continuing to catch their breath. Cuniculus stood until a rustling sound caused her to run and hide under him, having a bit of fear in her still. All the while, Vulpes smiled at her with a bit of amusement, saying nothing but only chuckling. Her face pocked out, checking to ensure the threat had disappeared. "Oh wow, I feel embarrassed now." She crept out from under him and went where she thought her warren was. "Hate to think how getting back to the warren will be. I'll be starting all the way."

Solis was close to the horizon, only minutes away from setting fully. Taking a few steps, she heard Vulpes prance over to her quickly. "Sheila, wait, hold up a sec." He made it ahead of her, cutting her off.

She paused, her ears laying back at his sudden outburst. "I need to get home before it gets dark. What part of that did you not understand."

"It's just probably not a good idea to be wanderin' 'bout the woods on yer own. I'm not sayin' ya can't, just that it might not be in yer best interest."

"What am I to do? I can't just sleep out in the open. I'll be snatched or killed before morning. I know you mean well, but that's a terrible idea."

"Wha' if ya were to stay underground?"

"I could dig a scrap. It'll shelter me but not give me protection."

"I think I have an idea, but I don't know if ya'll like it."

"What is it? I'm all ears, dearie." Cuniculus flickered her long ears playfully, seeing his head cock in confusion. "Sorry, it's a little joke my family says whenever someone asks that."

He chuckled but wanted to be taken seriously. "Since it's getting' dark, and there seems to be no other place to go. Well, I-I was wonderin' if ya would like to maybe stay in my den? Ya could leave when Solis comes up, but I don't want to be weird or pushy."

"Oh, do you care for my safety that much, Vulpes? I don't want to be a burden."

"No, it's no trouble at all. After all, who says we can't help each other out?"

"You do have a point there," said Cuniculus, rubbing the ground with her paw.

"It's all up to ya, of course. I don't want ya to feel uncomfortable."

His cheeks seemed redder than usual, making her wonder if he had the same feeling she did. "I could stay in your den this evening. One night can't hurt."

With a small sound, he nodded. "Wow, didn't think ya'd agree to that."

"It's not like you're going to eat me, darling, right?" She nudged him, feeling his solid body never budge.

"No, I don't really like rabbits, too much fluff."

"So, where do you live?" asked Cuniculus, looking around. "Is it close by, I hope?"

"Not too far. This way, follow me and stay close. I wouldn't want ya to get lost or taken. Unless ya know where ya are, the forest can be dangerous for a prey animal."

"Don't need to tell me twice, darling." She smiled and felt her cheeks get warm again. Why did she have this weird sensation? How come it only happened when Vulpes said something nice? She shook the thought and trailed after him.

Vulpes walked while Cuniculus hopped beside him. He didn't go too fast, keeping a steady pace with her. They went into unknown territory by Cuniculus. The dark area put her on edge. She didn't want to get caught by an owl that flew overhead, screeching loudly. He was her only protection from the creatures of the night, so she made sure to stick by him.

"Hey, ya okay? Yer shakin' like a branch in the wind. Haven't ya ever been around these parts?"

"Look, I'm just not used to traveling by night. So, say no more about it, darling."

"No problem. By the way, why didn't ya run back there? I thought that's wha' yer kind did when faced with an enemy?"

"We fight if we have to. We're not complete wimps."

"I didn't mean it like that. All I meant was ya could've been captured again. Why risk it, yer freedom? All for, well, me?"

"I was feeling merciful," said Cuniculus, a small smirk followed.

"I had that one comin'. Guess I'm confused as to why ya helped me?"

"Well, I'm surprised myself. I suppose I felt I couldn't leave you behind to endure any more of that terrible place on your own."

"Well, thank ya."

"So, are we just goin' to stand here, or will you show me where you live?"

"Right, right, this way." He led the way, holding shrubs and limbs aside for her. "Hate to keep ya waitin' any longer, else ye might yell at me."

They traveled for a while through a meadow and up a few ridges. Coming upon a creek; it was too deep for her to swim across. Thus, Vulpes let her ride on his back, paddling across with ease. On the far bank, she leaped down and kept her gaze upon the creek. Drawn from her thoughts when Vulpes shook, wetting her with droplets.

"Vulpes!"

"Aye, yer fine, Sheila."

She moved her paw across her fur, seeing the water collect and float before her. It took her by surprise, uncertain how she could do such a thing. "V-Vulpes, look at this."

Vulpes paused in mid-step, turning back. With perked ears and an open muzzle, he was shocked to find Cuniculus controlling a ball of water. She waved her paw back and forth before her, moving it from left to right. Vulpes' eyes lit up, and he jumped and tried to grab it in his mouth. The liquid orb broke, wetting him. He tried to find where it went, lifting his front paws off the ground. "Wha' did ya do with it, Sheila?"

"Nothing, it was water. I moved it, somehow."

"Can ya do it again?"

She held her paw out, shutting her eyes and focusing her mind on the river. The steady flow, the very motion, felt a part of her, or was she merging with it? Taking in a sense, she took a deep breath. Slowly, the water level rose higher in the air.

"Sheila, that's amazin'!" Vulpes was unable to believe what he saw, glancing at Cuniculus. She slumped down, the water sinking back into the creek. "Luna's light, that was unbelievable. Wonder if I can do that." Vulpes went over and lifted his paw, trying to move it. But to no avail; the water was unresponsive. With a grunt, he turned from it. "Must not like me."

"Maybe it's different. I don't fully get it, but it's sort of falling into place." Her mind went back to their escape. "The rock, I think you did that."

"Who can say."

"You're not at all concerned? We might very well be on the verge of something amazing."

With a shrug of his shoulders, he tilted his head from left to right. "We'll figure it out later."

"If you say so."

They left the river bed and made their way deeper into the forest. After some time, they came to a hill where a lone tree stood. Seeing his home for the first time in so long, Vulpes stopped to admire it for a moment. "There she is, ain't she a beaut. Gives me shade in the summer and dry from the rain. A perfect place to call home."

"Looks cozy enough."

A breeze swooshed through the branches that danced back and forth up the slope they went. At the top, she could see the woods, fields, and rolling hills. For Cuniculus, it felt like she was among the stars and Luna.

"I must admit, dear, this is amazing. Your den is in a perfect area. I'm surprised you were smart enough to find such a spot." She threw him a quick wink, wanting him to know she wasn't serious.

"I try." He entered the hole that led down the slack run and into the den.

She felt his tail and trailed behind him, entering the opening. It was twice the size of the slack run in their warren. Then again, he was twice her size. Then it hit her. Did he build it for a family?

"Don't tell me you're the proud father of six pups? I never pegged you for the family fox." Vulpes stopped, and she bumped into his fluffy tail. Trying to look him in the face, she wanted to know why he halted all of a sudden. "Something the matter, darling?"

"I'm no father. Ya have to mate to have offspring." Though he smiled, it was fake, hiding a sad expression, no doubt.

"But, back at the steel room, you said that you were *'very popular among the vixens.'*"

"I lied. I only said it to make myself feel better. Truth is, I never had any luck when it came to courtship."

"Then why build a den? Why waste your time on such a big project, dearie?"

"I thought if I already dug the den, that a vixen would choose me over some chump," Vulpes answered with a laugh. "Didn't work, though, so I guess I'm the chump."

"Vulpes, I-" started Cuniculus.

"Ya were right 'bout me. I'm just a red-furred fool."

"You couldn't be more wrong, darling. Besides, being alone can't be all bad. You don't have to worry about taking care of others. All you have to do is look after yourself. You're lucky from my point of view." She smiled and found it nice to not be crowed, to be neck and neck with family members. "It's so peaceful, roomy, very refreshing."

"It's nice here. But it gets really cold on winter nights when there's only one body to warm the place. I wouldn't expect ya to know wha' I'm talkin' 'bout."

"At least being alone, no one can hurt you. In your story, the predators went after the weaker of the group. Someone like me." Cuniculus tilted her head to her left shoulder. "You say I don't know loneliness, but I understand it quite well, better than you think."

"Oh, right." Vulpes glanced at her missing front paw, forgetting numerous times she didn't have it. "I'm sorry, I can never remember that."

"It's fine, flattering, actually. Reliving compared to those who took one glance and pitied me like I'm some helpless doe who needs saving." She brushed it off like she always did. "Bucks see me as only half, choosing one who is more than I, fearful I may produce unnatural kids. These ears pick up on a good deal, even the hushed conversation behind my back."

"Jeez, and here I thought I was the one who had a hard life."

"I learned at a young age that I was on my own, that no one was going to make me happy. I had to do that for myself. It's something you'll have to learn as well, Vulpes." Her confident smile fell to a normal one. "I act high and mighty to hide the pain, pretending so no one knows."

"So, ya chose to be alone?"

"For the most part, I'm comfy with my life, free and unattached. I think you're looking at your life wrong. If you have a few who love you, you don't need a mate to be happy or to feel whole. That comes from discovering yourself and who you are, embracing it, and accepting it. Like me, dearie."

"Wow. No one's ever said such things to me before. Not even my mom gave me this kinda pep talk. Thanks, Sheila. I feel better."

"Vulpes, you're not alone anymore." She moved closer to him, wanting him to see her words matched her action.

"That means a lot to me, more than ya could know."

Realizing her paw was on his much larger one, she flushed and pulled away. "Well, umm, let's get some shut-eye. I'm rather tired after today."

"Yeah, I'll see ya tomorrow mornin'." There they were, lying close and drifting off to sleep.

CHAPTER X:

To Lie and Hide

During the night, Cuniculus groaned and thrashed, dreaming of the monster. The world was dark. Only the monster could be seen, reaching out to grab her. She ran and saw Vulpes attacking the monster and giving up his freedom for her. The monster glowed red, taking hold of Vulpes and bending his body to break his bones. The cracks were terrible, but nothing compared to his screams of agony. Terror filled her, for the dream was so real, to the point where she thought he was going to die.

She gasped and sat up, waking in Vulpes' den. The large den was held up by a tree root, and beside her was Vulpes, alive and well. He stood over her, searching her with concern. "Ya, okay?"

"It was a dream, yet it felt so real. The monster was there, you, and I was so afraid." She trailed off, taking a shaky breath. "He was going to kill you."

"Me?"

"Yes, he captured you after we escaped, and I could do nothing to help. I am weak." She shook and sobbed into her paw, unable to keep it together.

"No, no, that's not true, ya are tough, Sheila." His nose brushed her cheek, wiping the tears from it. "Ya endured that terrible place, kept me goin' with yer positive outlook. Ya didn't break, and that tells me ya are strong."

"Smooth talking fox." She burrowed into him, feeling his front leg wrap around and hold her close. It felt safe to be in his hold, familiar in some way. "Thank you."

His paw rubbed her back, soothing her. "Figures I'd be the one to die first, though. I gotta say, I'm a little hurt by that."

"Always thinking of yourself, darling." She chuckled and sat back, wiping a tear from her eye. With a few sniffs, she collected herself. "How embarrassing. Me allowing you to see me in this way."

"Ya saw the valuable me."

Running her paw to his fur, she spoke softly. "Will you lay by me?"

"If it will get ya to not wake me again. I gotta have my beauty sleep."

"You're such a jerk."

"But I'm yer jerk."

"Yes," said Cuniculus, brushing her face into him. "My jerk."

She lay down, and he settled beside her, tail wrapping around to pull her close. Nuzzling near him, she brushed her paw along his fur. He reached out and held her in his arms, nuzzling down and smiling with comfort. As they slept, the watches glowed yellow, showing the pair were happy.

By late evening, Vulpes woke, hearing a voice bounce off the den walls. "Vulpes." Wondering if he were half asleep, he blinked and listened carefully. "Find me." The voice, he knew it, sensed her somehow. It belonged to the monster female. But who was she? Why did she feel like family when he'd never met such a creature?

"Sheila!" called Vulpes, making his way to Cuniculus' slumbering form. "Wake up. Did ya hear that?"

Cuniculus rose, and wondered what happened. His eyes were wide, gazing at her with shock. "What's wrong now?"

"Ya didn't hear that voice?" said Vulpes. "It was the monster from our vision. I knew her too like a father knows his daughter and-"

"Vulpes, I think you were having a nightmare." Rubbing her eyes, she curled back down. "Now, lay down, dearie, and let's sleep."

"Yer right must be left over fear from our time back in that horrible place."

"I think it will take time to realize this is not a dream, that we're free." She gave him a sympathetic smile, knowing he was suffering the aftereffect of where they'd been and what they'd seen. What made it a bit easier to get through was that they had each other. Even if it only lasted a night, she'd treasure it. "Don't fret, dearie. I'm here."

"As am I, all ya got to do is glance over yer shoulder, and there I'll be."

"I run, you chase." She whispered.

"Ya run, I chase."

She sighed, feeling Vulpes lay down and wrap his body around her. As he lay, he couldn't help but think of the monster female's words. Find me. Who was she? Why did she want to speak to him? Did she know the monster? So many questions.

The next morning Cuniculus slept in a ball curled up against Vulpes, whose body surrounded her. Burrowing into him, he purred against her, sleeping soundly in the warm cozy den. She slowly opened her eyes at the sudden movement, glancing about with a sleepy gaze. Her tiny paw rubbed her eyes, clearing the sleep from them. She patted his nose, watching him wake.

"Morning Vulpes, ready for something to eat?"

"I sure am. For now, I shall dine on ya for breakfast."

"Nice try, but I'm not buying it."

"Maybe this will change yer mind." He licked her ears playfully, pinning her down. She laughed and batted him away, feeling his long tongue lick her face. Pausing for a moment, he pulled back quickly. "Sorry, did I hurt ya? I wasn't gonna eat ya."

"Oh really." Leaping up, she crawled up his shoulders, straddling his neck. She rubbed her paw along his ears, feeling him mellow out. He purred, enjoying the sensation. His stomach growled suddenly, echoing through the den. They froze, not moving a muscle. "Hopefully, you won't eat me." With a chuckle, he rolled over, Cuniculus moving from his back to his chest. She rubbed it, making his left hind leg move. "Wow, what's with that?"

"Oh, it's involuntary. When ya brush my stomach, my leg automatically does that. Well, maybe we could get some food."

With a nod, she hopped off and headed to the slack run. Vulpes wasn't too far behind, and they crawled out onto the grass. Wildflowers grew in patches, and bees buzzed around to collect honey. Cuniculus' nose twitched, and she hopped about, seeking out the best grass to eat. Finding a nice cluster of clover, she took a big bite and tasted the dew-soaked leaves. It gave the greens a moist texture, making her sigh with joy. Vulpes went around marking his territory, and she continued eating, her ears flat on her back.

When Vulpes finished his business, he came over to sit beside her, having something on his mind. "So, this is probably goodbye forever, eh?" His voice was soft, not angry, just low. "Ya said it yerself, that after we escaped, we should go our separate ways."

"I know what I said." It was her time to be honest, to share her true feelings. "I deeply regret it."

"Ya do?" Ears perked; he was taken aback by her response.

"The truth is, Vulpes, I enjoyed our time together and wish for it to continue. Unless you don't want to."

Seeing her nose twitch and eyes get glassy, he scrambled to speak. "No, no! Of course, I want to see ya. I just didn't think ya'd want to see me again, that's all."

"Of course, I want to see you. Maybe I could visit you again?"

"Around dusk, perhaps? And if it gets too dark yer welcome to stay over again, yeah?" asked Vulpes playfully.

"I'd like that, dearie, very much." Agreed, Cuniculus, in a playful tone.

"Will I see ya later then?"

"I'll see you around." She tilted her head up, seeing him lean down to nuzzle her nose. "Farewell, for now, Vulpes dear."

"Farewell, Sheila."

With a smile, she turned and left. He watched with a soft expression, seeing her disappear into the brush.

Giving a small sigh, he was glad he'd continue to see her again. Cuniculus, the rabbit who made him her prey.

Cuniculus made her way home, feeling her heart race with anticipation and excitement. Soon she'd reunited with her loved ones, the family she never thought she'd see again. Several of the warren's members grazed along the hillside while the kittens hopped about, playing and rolling through the grass. The sight melted her heart, making her eyes grow moist with tears of joy.

"Look! She's back!" hollered one, noticing her along the edge of the woodland.

They turned from their grazing to gather into a group, waiting for her. She hopped up to them with a bright smile, glad to see them again. Out from the group came Diana.

"Mother," whispered Cuniculus.

"Where have you been, darling?" Speaking between sobs, Diana feared the worst for her daughter. "We thought you were dead. I thought I lost you to the Lands Beyond."

Others began to sniff her over, hoping to find out where she'd been the whole time. Diana nuzzled Cuniculus when one of her siblings made a face of disgust. The individual shook his head and leaned in to get another sniff. "What in the warren, Cuniculus! You stink of a fox!"

She moved away from him, trying to shelter herself from the curious eyes and noses surrounding her. Seeing them come closer and closer, she felt claustrophobic. "I had a run-in with one, but I got away. Don't worry, my darlings. I had it all under control."

"Yeah, right, no one ever survives a run-in with one of the hundred, especially if it's a fox."

"Well, I did."

She pressed herself against the ground, trying to make herself seem smaller, hoping the others would leave her be. They came near, surrounding her in a circle of fluff, wanting to get a whiff of her.

"Oh, give her some room. I'm sure she's tired from her journey." Diana shushed them back, the group obeying and leaving her be. "Come along, dear. I'll groom you, and you can tell me all about your adventure."

"Of course, Mother, I'd be happy to spend one-on-one with you after such a long time."

They went to the warren's opening and went down the tunnels through the darkness until they arrived at Cuniculus' burrow. Diana groomed Cuniculus, cleaning her fur till it was silky smooth. Being groomed was intimate for animals, only done between family members or a mated pair.

"So, where have you been?"

"Where have I been?" repeated Cuniculus, stalling till she thought of the answer. "Well, I was out grazing when I chased a buck about to this odd-looking place. There we came across a monster. Neither I nor the male had ever seen such a creature and froze with fear. He captured us and put us in a dreadful place where we couldn't get outside at all. I have no idea how long we were there, but it was awful."

"Sounds just horrible. However, did you get away?"

"Well, the buck told me to chew through this black thing, and we escaped. Now here I am, though I will remain friends with him."

Cuniculus hated to lie to Diana, but she didn't want to worry her about her friendship with a predator. Diana brightened up when hearing about the buck, glad that Cuniculus might've found a suitable male to possibly mate with.

"Why honey, that's wonderful. I was worried that you would never find a nice buck to settle down with. All your siblings thought you'd be single your whole life. Is he a handsome buck?" Diana smiled, patting Cuniculus with excitement. "What does he look like?"

Cuniculus felt her cheeks heat. Even just thinking about Vulpes brought forth a warm sensation. Though her stomach flipped, she spoke calmly. "He has red fur and sky-blue eyes. Oh, Mother, they are lovely. He's such a dear too. Polite and respectful, I might add."

"Will we be able to meet him anytime soon?"

Cuniculus chuckled a worried laugh. "He lives far away. When we meet, we meet in the middle."

"Solis above this is wonderful. Do you think you'll mate with him?"

"Mother!" exclaimed Cuniculus with shock.

"You are a year-old darling, and I'd like some grandkids out of you. After all, most of your siblings have a few litters."

"Mother, you have at least a dozen grandkids from my other siblings, I think you can wait a little longer. Besides, we're just friends."

Cuniculus saw Diana's happiness fad replaced with sorrow. "We were so very worried about you, you know."

"I'm just glad to be back at the warren."

Cuniculus nuzzled her head on Diana's shoulder, feeling her eyes well up with tears. Diana nuzzled her back, sniffing slightly. Once they collected themselves, they pulled apart and left the burrow to eat with the others.

Outside, Cuniculus' siblings spoke in hushed tones. Going back and forth, they worried the fox might show up and dig them out. They became silent when Cuniculus appeared out of the warren's opening, staring at her with wide eyes and twitching noses. She smiled shyly before eating, wondering why they seemed on edge. As for the group, they shared worried expressions, trying to act as though nothing were wrong.

CHAPTER XI:

Hold Your Breath

Deep in the woods, near Vulpes' den, a clear stream ran through the forest. Along the edge, he came out of the brush and walked over to the river's shore. He leaned down and lapped the water, enjoying the creek he'd missed. The water tasted more natural than the kind he drank back at the monster's place. With his back to the wood, a shadow fell over him, yet he continued to lap the water calmly.

"Hey Eve, how are ya doin'?" A light red vixen walked silently up behind him. Her silver eyes looked him over as if she'd seen a ghost, making her blink several times. Giving her a coy grin, he arched a brow. "Sis, ya okay?"

"I haven't seen you around. Lately, I thought you were dead," Eve answered, eyes welling with tears. "Where have you been? I spent many nights trying to find you. I even had Deva look for you."

Deva was a raccoon whom Eve planned to be mates will. Last Vulpes checked, that was the plan. "How is the girlfriend?"

"She left."

"Why? I thought ya two were goin' to be together?"

"She left with a set of sibling sheep, convinced a danger was coming to their section of woods and meadows." There was a pause before she went on. "I tracked you to a strange clearing, but the unfamiliar smells caused me to turn back. Is that where you've been this whole time?"

"I'm back now. That's all that matters." Vulpes stepped close to the creek, avoiding his sister's curious gaze. She was about to speak when another voice cut in.

"Vulpes, back from the dead." A male fox stepped out, with green eyes and a husky build. "You've been gone for many days and nights, reeking of prey. Would you care to share what happened?"

"Hello, Reed. Good to see ya too."

"I'll cut to the chase. Did you catch that, doe?"

His eyes were sharp, tail flickering behind him. If anyone could see through Vulpes' lie, it'd be Reed. Vulpes swallowed a few times, thinking about what to say. "Wha' do ya think happened?" Answering another question might buy him more time to come up with a better excuse.

"Don't tell me, did those cute little bunnies capture you?" Reed retorted with a bit of smugness.

"Yeah, and I think I'm mated to their queen."

"Don't get smart with me, you cocky little snip."

"Then don't get in my face, mate."

The pair growled, fur fluffing. They were different in temperament and often disagreed on several occasions, fighting from the time they learned to talk. The air was thick, and Eve glanced from one to the other, usually stopping them from going at it.

"That's enough, you two. We're not puppies anymore." Walking between them, she turned to Vulpes, knowing he'd back down before Reed. "We're adults, time to act like it."

"All right, I hear ya."

"Very well." Reed took a step back yet locked eyes with Vulpes. "So, did you eat the doe or not?"

"I almost had her."

"Almost. Interesting? You've been wanting to catch her since you we able to hunt. Now you're telling us she just got away? Seems kinda fishy."

"I messed up okay, Reed. I'm not a perfect hunter like ya are. Now if ya don't mind, I have things I need to do." Vulpes brushed by Reed quickly, strolling into the forest and leaving the bewildered pair behind.

With Vulpes gone, they were curious in a different way. Being the responsible one, Eve was concerned for Vulpes, feeling he was hiding something due to fear of judgment. "He's acting weird."

Reed, of course, spoke his mind and didn't care whom it hurt. "Maybe one of us should follow him and see what he's up to." Reed got ready to head into the woods after Vulpes when something held him back, keeping him in place. Eve's paw stood on his tail, preventing him from following Vulpes. "Hey, what gives, Eve?"

"He'll tell us sooner or later." Eve removed her paw from his tail, seeing him snatch and brush it out. "Be patient, he'll come around."

"Yeah, right, knowing Vulpes, he'll take the truth to the Lands Beyond with him."

She shot Reed a warning glare. "Brother, don't keep at Vulpes about the doe. You might push him away from us."

"It's always my fault, isn't it? You always took his side over mine, that no good, poor excuse for a hunter-"

"That's enough, Reed."

"You act like the oldest, but you're not. I am-"

"Then behave like it for a change. I'll see you around." She trotted off across the creek, leaping from rock to rock. Reed snorted and left into the woods while Solis hung high in the air.

Cuniculus was on the hillside, basking in the warmth from Solis. The day became night, and Cuniculus smiled brightly, going to let Diana know she was leaving for the evening. She made her way through the woods, moving faster than ever before. Wind aided her, for she was able to control the air around her, assisting her to hop in large leaps. It must've been yet another gift from the object, allowing her to easily wield it. With a powerful blast, up she went, able to see over the top of the trees. The leaves danced from the gust, dust swirling below where she once was. It was breathtaking, sweeping over the land like a bird. The feeling was freeing, making her smile with glee.

Coming down, she struck the earth hard and saw the hill come into view, surprised by how quickly she got there. "Boy, what a useful gift to have." Shooting ahead, not only was she able to fly but race speedily from one spot to another. "Vulpes, you're not going to believe this!"

She hopped up the hill and found him waiting, accidentally bumping into his head due to how fast she approached him. They fell back and rubbed their sore foreheads, trying to stop the pain.

"I'm glad ya came. I wasn't too sure if ya'd come." His tail wagged back and forth, unable to contain his joy.

"I'm able to use wind. I soared in great bounds."

He shook his head, unable to believe the news. "That's wonderful. I told ya, ya were strong."

Her smile changed, and she lowered her ears. "There is one other thing. My family asked about what happened. They wondered where I was and whom I met."

His ears perked, speaking nervously. "Wha' did ya tell 'em?"

"I told them about being captured and a little bit about you."

"Luna above, how did they feel 'bout that? They probably dropped dead hearin' that ya were friends with me."

Rubbing her paw in the dirt, she cleared her throat. "Well, I kinda told them you were a buck." She looked worriedly at Vulpes, who was thoughtful for a moment.

"Does that mean I can tell my friends yer a vixen?"

"I'm serious. We do need to worry about how we smell, Vulpes. My siblings detected your scent on me. I fear our friendship could lead to danger."

"I know wha' ya mean, my brother wondered where I'd been. He asked why I didn't eat y-" Vulpes stopped, unable to complete his sentence.

"Why you hadn't killed me? The scent is a problem."

"All we have to do is think of how to hide the scent."

"I think that's easier said than done, Vulpes."

Rubbing a paw to his chin, a gesture he found himself doing unlike before. It was silly, but it helped him think clearly, giving him a good idea. "I've got it! We'll wash in the river before we see our friends or family. It will not only keep us clean but protect us from their questions."

"That's a fabulous idea, darling. Why didn't I think of it?"

"Perhaps those things helped me think better."

"Those objects. By the way, have you noticed something different about yourself?" She glanced down at herself, then at him. "Those things did this to us. If only we knew more about them."

Vulpes gave a small nod, meeting her soft brown eyes. "The night ya slept here, a girl spoke to me. She told me to find her. I think the monster, Sheila, might be able to help us understand how all this happened."

"How do we find this female?"

Vulpes glanced around as if hoping the answer would come. Yet, he hadn't the faintest clue. "I'm not sure. But perhaps if we use our abilities more, we'll grow stronger. Might lead us to her."

"Wow, another good idea. That's two in a row. That's a record for you." She gave him a nuzzle, feeling his thick fur along her nose.

Taking in her warm scent, he went to lie down. "We'll figure it out tomorrow."

CHAPTER XII:

The Change

From that evening on, they continued to meet secretly by night, washing in the river before parting ways the next morning. The days became weeks, and the weeks became months as the forbidden friends continued to see each other and learn about their powers. Cuniculus found she could attach water to her missing limb, replacing and swinging from branch to branch, using her air to fly. Vulpes figured earth was his gift, along with fire, placing it around his body and joining Cuniculus in the air. They were changing, noticing their reflections in the water they drank at. They stood on their hind legs rather than all fours, finding the old way of walking to feel odd and out of place. Even their paws looked more human-like, with opposable thumbs and flickering fingers.

Cuniculus was the first to notice their changes, voicing her discovery. "Vulpes darling, do we seem different?"

Vulpes peered down at the water, seeing their reflection. "I see a good-lookin' fox and cute bunny."

"I'm serious." Said Cuniculus, batting his arm playfully. "We're becoming more like him, the monster."

"We'll never be like him."

"How do you know? The power, it might turn us dark, make us bad."

Vulpes lifted her chin, brushing her cheek with his other paw. "That could never happen. Because, unlike him, we use our abilities for good."

"Perhaps you're right."

"I usually am."

"That's a good one, darling."

They left the area, making their way to Vulpes' den. The more they used it, the better they got. Still, they hadn't been able to contact the monster female, uncertain if they'd ever be able to communicate with her. Nevertheless, they kept the whole powers to themselves. Well, Vulpes never told his family of his newfound skills. Cuniculus, on the other paw, would use her powers to entertain the kittens when the other family members weren't watching, keeping them busy and out of trouble.

"Aunt Cuniculus! Aunt Cuniculus! Do the trick, do the trick!" Called the kittens, surrounding her and brushing her with their noses.

Cuniculus made sure the adults weren't around, using her paw to control a vortex of wind. Lifting a leaf, she moved it around for the kittens to chase, hearing them laugh. It gave her joy to see their amazement, hopping up and down with glee. They went for it, heading into the woods. Cuniculus followed, sliding down some ice to gain ground. Coming to a clearing, wind surrounded them, shooting up more leaves. The kittens were so busy playing with the raining leaves that they were unaware someone was watching.

Cuniculus gasped when she heard a growl and gathered the kittens behind her, keeping them between herself and the unknown predator. "Kids, stay behind me." They obeyed, shaking and looking at where the rustle came from.

From behind a tree, a pair of wolves emerged. One was a large male with black and white fur and cunning brown eyes. The other was a female with green eyes; her fur was black as night. Unlike the male, her disposition was meek and nervous, hunched slightly.

"Well, well, look what we have here, Lomasi, a nice meal of rabbits."

"You stay away from us, or else!"

"Oh, prey that talks back. You sure have guts." With a half grin, he licked his chops. "I can't wait to taste them."

"Kittens, run. I'll hold them off."

They did as Cuniculus said, fleeing back to the warren. The male wolf nudged the female to follow them. She slowly walked in the direction, only to be lifted and twisted in a sea of wind. Her world spun, sending her back to the earth.

"What in Luna's name?" The male turned from the down female to Cuniculus, who stood on her hind legs, paw raised. "What are you?"

"Why don't you come over and find out, darling."

"Don't mind if I do." With bared fangs, the wolf leaped forward. Before he could even bite her, the wind shot up and gut-punched him, sending him sprawling to the ground. The rabbit pulled water from a nearby puddle and attached it to her missing left shoulder, waving like an extremely long arm. The tip wrapped around the rock, and next, a twig, tossing them at him. Rolling over, he paused when she halted for a moment. "I suggest you leave."

The female wolf went to the male, nudging him with wide eyes. "Hey, Demetri, I-I-I think we s-should do as she s-says."

"Shut the cuss up. Did I ask for your opinion?"

"N-no."

"Then don't speak."

Glancing between him and the doe, her eyes were wide and fearful. "I mean, she's k-kinda strong, for p-prey that is."

"I don't care. We will not be bested by food."

"If you s-say so."

"Attack!" He charged, feeling the water whip him across the nose. With a whimper from the sting, he saw the rabbit dash for a tangled mess of briers. Growling, he glared at Lomasi, who only shrugged. "Now look what you've done. You let her get away."

"Me, w-what did I do? I did n-nothing."

"Precisely. You're useless and are lucky we don't eat you instead. The only reason we keep you around is to flesh out prey. Now get in there and find her."

She was hesitant to go, shaking her head from side to side. "I-I don't know. The last time I went into a tight area like t-that, I got this f-funky smelling stuff on my fur. Took weeks t-to wash out."

Demetri met her nervous gaze with a frown. "If you don't get in there, my foot will be up your rear. Now you decide what you want?"

"Fine." She crawled into the thick brier, feeling the thorns prick her skin. Her fur got caught, forcing her to crawl on her stomach. "T-the things I d-do for family."

"Quite complaining, and hurry up," Demetri spoke gruffly from outside the briar patch.

Before she knew it, she fell downward, tumbling between a set of rocks. It was a tiny craves, covered by brush. Wider at the top, it got tighter the farther down it went, pinning Lomasi's body. She struggled and couldn't get out, being caught between a rock and a hard place, literally.

"Demetri, help! I-I-I'm stuck!" She cried out, not moving out of fear of falling farther and being crushed. "D-Demetri!"

"Don't worry!" Demetri yelled from afar, clearly not going in after her. "I'll get the pack and return shortly to help you out."

"Wait, d-don't leave me!" Called Lomasi, hearing paws rush away. "Demetri? D-Demetri!"

Lomasi trembled, shaking and panting with fear. Tears welled in her eyes, and she figured he wouldn't come back for her, leaving her to die. A flash moved across the opening, the rabbit climbing down to her.

"Hang on, dearie. I'm coming to help you."

"What, w-why?"

"Because it's what's right. Now keep still, lest you fall and get stuck even worse." Said Cuniculus politely, moving down under her trapped form. "I'll have you out in a moment."

"W-what, how?" Suddenly, Lomasi felt the air from below.

Cuniculus blew wind up, trying to push her out. Though, the large female didn't budge, remaining caught while the breeze blew through her fur. Cuniculus used ice to create a slippery surface to attempt to shoot Lomasi out. When that didn't work, she knew only Vulpes' earth power could save the wolf.

"I'm going to get help-"

"Y-you're not going to leave m-me, are you?"

"Perhaps, not." Cuniculus raised her paw, and a single flake of snow flew off. "I might be able to send Vulpes a message." All they could do was hold tight, hoping Cuniculus' plan would work.

The flake went through the woods, going to Vulpes. It reached the den, finding him curled up. The single flake danced around and tugged his tail, trying to wake him.

"Stop that bug." Vulpes groaned and turned over, batting the flake, sending it spinning. It got control and landed on his nose, causing him to stir and wake. He was confused, seeing the flake bounce up and down at the tip of his muzzle. Blinking, he wondered if he were still asleep. When he smelled a hint of Cuniculus' scent, he realized it was sent from her. Rising to his feet, he kept his eyes on it. "Where's Cuniculus?"

The flake left, Vulpes racing after it. He followed it, making his way into the forest. Seeing a tangled mess of briers, he picked up Cuniculus' scent, and a pair of wolves. Fearing the worst, he burst into flames. A small path was burnt, put out once he had enough room. He found the craves, peering down to see a wolf.

"Aye, who are ya?" Not seeing Cuniculus, he hoped the she-wolf didn't eat her. "If ya hurt Cuniculus, I'll crush ya like a bug."

"The n-names Lomasi, are you V-Vulpes by any chance?"

"Yeah, that's my name." With confusion, he cocked his head sideways. "H-how do ya know my name?"

"Vulpes dear, do you think you could get her out?" Cuniculus' voice called from below.

"Cuniculus, ya aren't hurt?"

"No, now see if you can remove her from this place. Hate for her to fall and injure herself."

"Sure, don't move, Miss Lomasi."

Vulpes raised his paws, moving the rock just enough for Lomasi to move. Cuniculus quickly sent a blast of wind, firing Lomasi out of the craves like a shot. She flew and, before she could hit the ground, was caught and gently set down.

On the ground, she sat up and looked at the pair. "A f-fox and rabbit, working t-together? Wow, I have s-seen it all."

"Are you all right, darling?" asked Cuniculus, looking her over. "You seem fine."

"I'm g-great, thanks to the pair of you. How can I-I ever thank you?"

"By not returning to my warren again."

"I-I can agree to that." Said Lomasi, giving a small bow of respect. "Well, I'll g-get back to my p-pack so they don't come looking for m-me."

"Take care of yerself." Vulpes saw her leave, turning to Cuniculus. "So, want me to walk ya the rest of the way to yer warren."

"I'll be fine, thank you, Vulpes dear. I'll see you later, though."

"Yeah, see ya."

He saw her leave, wishing he could go with her. But her family, they'd never allow it, wouldn't want a fox among them. Standing for a moment, he saw her join her family members. They looked happy, huddling around Cuniculus to talk. With lowered ears, he turned to go back to his den, knowing he'd see her later that evening.

Part Three:

I Chose You

CHAPTER XIII:

Tension

Though it seemed her family greeted her, it was the opposite. She was met with many angry expressions, giving them a coy grin. Her siblings stood by their crying kittens, who told them about the wolves. "Care to tell us why you led our children into danger."

Cuniculus raised her head, going to them. "I can explain all of this."

"How could you be so careless? They could've been killed."

"I distracted the wolves for them to escape-"

"If you wish to watch them, you will stay close to the warren."

"Agreed, no more adventures beyond the warren." Cuniculus lowered her head, feeling bad for worrying them. "I promise."

They turned and took the kittens into the warren, leaving Diana and Cuniculus. Diana sighed and went to Cuniculus, nuzzling her. "Come dearie, let's graze together." They were along the hill, enjoying the stillness, till Diana spoke. "So dear, have you two mated yet?"

Cuniculus about spit up, and a piece of grass hung out of her mouth. She swallowed hard and stared back, wondering what Diana was talking about. "Mother!"

"It's just I can't wait to see their colors. I wonder what is more dominant, red or tan?" Diana went on despite Cuniculus' dismay. "Dear, you're not getting any younger. You're over two years old, old enough to create your own legacy."

"Mother! I-We're not ready for that." She tugged her ears down, hoping Diana would talk about a different topic. For if it was one thing Diana enjoyed more than tending to others, it was admiring a new litter of kittens. After Diana could not reproduce kids of her own, she eagerly waited till each of her daughters gave birth. Whatever the case, it made Cuniculus flush, not interested in mating or baring kittens. At least, not yet, perhaps even ever.

"Dear, you've been seeing him for quite some time. Mating is more than just for producing. It's for sharing a special moment in time, a bond that unites you as mates for life. I want you to be happy. I know you are when you're with him." Cuniculus froze, listening to Diana's soft voice. "I've seen a big difference in you. You're stronger and more confident in yourself. I'm proud to see you grow so much over the past year. And I think he's helped you with that."

Cuniculus grinned, knowing it probably had more to do with the watch than with Vulpes. Though she wouldn't dare tell Diana. Why, she found it hard to fully accept herself. Not to mention the only one who understood was Vulpes, for he was the only witness to the monster, the horrible place. They shared so much and grew together.

"You think so?"

"Yes, you care deeply for him. I see it in your eyes and hear it in your voice when you talk about him. I'm glad you found someone who makes you as happy as he does. I only wish I could meet him."

"Mother, I told you he can't be far from his warren. He travels a long way just to see me. I hate for him to have to make the dangerous hick here."

"Well, you could always make a new warren between here and there. Then we could meet him. Oh, I'm sure he'd be glad to meet us as well. Have you told him of us?"

"Yes, and I wish you could. I do." She felt guilty, knowing she couldn't ever let her family meet him. Knowing better, for they wouldn't accept a predator among them.

"You two seem good for each other."

"Yeah, truth be told, I want him to be a big part of my life. I'd like to do more than spend the night with him. It would be nice to spend more time with him." It was here. Cuniculus didn't know if she was telling Diana about the fake buck or the real Vulpes. "But I don't know if he'll want to be with me. I mean, well, you know."

"Darling, he must not mind what you look like. He likes you for who you are, which is very important, more important than appearances. Intimacy is fine, but you must be able to talk and share your feelings with them. If he cares about you the way you said he does, I think he's more serious about it than you give him credit. It'll all work out, dear. You'll see." Diana nuzzled Cuniculus, and the two went back to eating in silence, enjoying the cool breeze that sent a wave over the grass.

In the woods by the stream, Vulpes walked out from the shrubs. He itched his ear, feeling prickly from the walk through the forest. Seeing his reflection in the water, a ripple changed it. There was a different face, the monster female. Vulpes was speechless upon hearing her voice. "Why haven't you tried to contact me? You must talk to me before it's too late."

A fish swam through the water, catching his attention. He shrugged it off, thinking it was merely his imagination playing a trick on him. He crouched down, waiting for the fish to come back around. His jaw clamped down, causing water to splash up from the prey's attempt to get away. Turning with his catch, he lay down to eat it, holding the wiggling fish between his paws.

From behind the hedgerow, Reed was hidden in shadow with a frown on his face. He walked out, having a crooked smile on his muzzle. "That doe comes here to wash, and I could catch it for you, split the food right down the middle."

"Will ya let it be, brother?"

"Gods above, Vulpes, I know she's been staying in your den!"

Silence followed; Vulpes drew his lips back and growled. "Oh, so ya've been spyin' on me, how low."

"Yes, you're lucky I didn't jump out and kill her. Honestly, I regret not tearing my claws into her."

"If ya try to hurt her, I'll attack ya."

"Why wait when we can finish this now?!?"

"What are ya, talkin'-" Before he could finish, Reed jumped him, clawing and biting. Vulpes yipped with pain, spinning around, trying desperately to throw Reed off his back. They stirred up dust in the tussle, and Vulpes managed to get back on his feet. Once the dust settled, they circled each other. Their hacks rose, and low growls filled the air. Vulpes knew he could unleash his powers onto Reed, yet knew it'd be wrong. The fight would be unfair, like how the monster overpowered him and Cuniculus. With a deep breath, he eyed Reed up. "If it's a fight ya want, it's a fight ya'll get!"

"Bring it on!"

Both pawed the ground, their tails swishing back and forth with fury. Before they fought further, paws landed between them, preventing them from leaping forward. Both sat back on their haunches and glanced up at the animal, curious who dared stand in their way. It was none other than their sister, seeing her through the cloud of dust. Her gaze was serious, staring down at them with shame.

"The sky and land, what is up with the two of you! Fighting like a pair of fools!" She turned from Reed to the bleeding Vulpes. Both dropped their heads, feeling foolish for having their sister break up their quarrel. "If I didn't intervene, would you have killed one another?"

"Maybe, I don't know." Reed glared Vulpes down, wiping the blood from his muzzle.

Lowering his gaze, Vulpes spoke. "That piece of chickweed questioned me 'bout the doe. All I said was it no longer mattered to me. He demanded I tell him more, and for not givin' him a reasonable explanation, he attacked me!"

"Don't make me the bad guy here. Honestly, I can't believe I'm saying this. But I'm worried about you, scared for your wellbeing."

All were silent for a moment, not sure how to react to what Reed said. He was never the kind to let his feeling be known to others, so when he showed he cared, it made them wonder.

"Thanks for yer concern, brother, but ya wouldn't understand. Ya might even hate me for it."

"Well, I might, depending on what you have to say."

A slap from Eve hushed Reed for Vulpes to speak. "Go on, we're listening."

He took a cool breath and told them how he and Cuniculus were captured. How they became friends over the awful ordeal, and what all they endured in captivity. The monster, their escape, everything but the watches, of course.

"There, that's wha' I've been holdin' back." Vulpes finished.

"Hold it, hold it. So, what you're saying is, you and the doe are friends?"

"If I said yes, would ya kill me?"

"Of course, not Vulpes. Whom you choose to befriend is up to you." She smiled warmly, glad he talked to them at long last. "Vulpes, do you like the doe as more than a friend?"

Vulpes felt a smile cross his face, feeling a warm sensation. It was like nothing he ever knew before, starting in his gut and going to his face. "Well, I can't imagine my life without her."

"What a dork!" Spat Reed out of the blue. "A doe and a fox as more than friends. I never heard of such a thing. You poor sapling, you must be desperate for a mate to use that doe as a replacement for a vixen!"

"You're such a jerk sometimes!" Eve frowned at Reed, who stopped laughing once she spoke. "Love is love, and we should support his decision to whom he wishes to be with."

"I'm just tellin' it like it is. Besides, did you even tell this prey about scent marking?"

"N-no, I haven't." Vulpes responded timidly.

"Well, tell her, and when she bolts to leave you alone, don't come crying to me. Do yourself a favor and move on. Find a nice vixen, and you'll be much happier." He smirked before going off into the forest, leaving the pair behind.

After he left, Vulpes thought over what Reed said. He let out a pitiful sigh, not knowing what to do next. "Reed's right."

"That's a first."

"I mean it, Eve. I haven't even tried to look for a mate or thought 'bout a vixen. I feel deeply for Cuniculus, no matter how different we are. I'm a fool to think she'd want me over some good-lookin' buck."

"Well, she must like you. Otherwise, she wouldn't continue to see you."

"Yer fine with me bein' interested in prey? Ya aren't gonna stop talkin' to me?"

"You can relax, Vulpes. I knew there was something on your mind by how you seemed to hold your breath when you were around us. But it's okay now. You can breathe. I love you, and I want you to go woo the doe of your dreams if it pleases you. Life's too short to keep your feelings to yourself."

"I never thought of it that way. Yer right, after all, who knows wha' tomorrow will bring. I could die and never get to tell Cuniculus how much I care 'bout her."

"Indeed, well, I wish you the best of luck. I'll see you later. Let me know how it goes."

"I will, thank ya, sis." He smiled at her and watched her leave. Alone, he thought about what his next step should be, knowing if there was time to share his feelings with Cuniculus.

CHAPTER XIV:

The Secrets We Keep

Cuniculus arrived at the den and entered to reach the bottom, where he pounced on her, licking her face playfully. Her back legs moved against his front legs, trying to push him off. He paused and burrowed his nose along her ears, enjoying how they moved. They stopped to catch their breath, meeting each other's gaze.

"My, aren't we happy this evening?" Cuniculus got to her feet and fixed her fur, brushing one of her ears. Taking a breath, she spoke. "Vulpes dear, I know this is an odd thing to ask, but have you ever thought about mating?"

"W-wha', matin'? With umm? With y-ya?"

"You know, mating with a vixen. Have you ever thought about it? I mean, with me being here, it will be impossible for you to find a mate. Isn't that what you wanted, dearie? A vixen who could give you a litter of pups to father."

"Oh, that. Well, not really. Why? Have ya thought 'bout findin' a nice bloke-buck to settle down with? Have lots of little kids jumpin' around?"

He imagined cute little fluff balls scurrying around the grass outside his den. Of course, he thought of pups, too, seeing Cuniculus and himself sitting side by side, watching their young play and frolic. Wait, his den? Their little ones? That could never happen. They couldn't even mate, let alone have offspring. He was lost in thought that he'd blocked out what she said.

"I'm sorry. Could ya repeat that I missed it?"

She sighed yet repeated what she had said earlier. "I don't know if I want a buck and a litter of kittens. It's so ordinary and dull. I was just curious as to what you wanted out of life?"

"Well, I'm happy with the way things are. Will I find a vixen? Who knows? Who cares. Ya seem happy with the way things are, yeah?"

"Yes, and I wouldn't change a thing. I wish we could spend the day together. There's so much we could do but can't."

With a small smile, he spoke softly. "I told my family 'bout you."

Ears shooting up, she turned to him with uncertainty. "What? How did they take it?"

"My sister took it well, my brother, not so much. But ya know wha'? I don't care. He nor anyone else can tell me whom I should spend my time with. And if I want to spend it with ya, then by the Gods, I will."

"I wish I were brave enough to tell the truth. But it's so hard. I mean it. My family is narrow-minded and won't understand. My worst fear is that they'll tell me to leave the warren."

"I know wha' ya mean, I thought my family would kill me. It's scary, yet it was worth it. Ya will get the chance, and when ya do, it'll work out."

"Ugh, now you sound like my Mother, Vulpes."

"I don't know wha' is worst. Bein' torn apart by my brother or bein' compared to yer Mother."

She hopped over and nuzzled him, silencing him from going on. They huddled close and soon drifted off to sleep. In Cuniculus' dream, she saw the monster again. The space around them was that of the forest, bright and beautiful as always, yet there was this odd feel to it. It came from the monster, that much she knew, ears flickering back. She stood on her hind legs, lifting her paw to fight back. "What do you want?"

"To display the extent of my powers." The monster walked closer, arms out as he glowed red. "Witness the destruction I can bring to your lush world, should I choose to."

She felt a shudder, eyes watching him closely. Lightening jumped from finger to finger, shooting out to destroy the land around them. Sparks flew while a fire burned out of control, and the world slowly changed. Flames surrounded her, yet she was unharmed. "Why would you do this?"

"Turn yourselves over by midnight the following evening or suffer the consequences." He didn't attack her, leaving space between them. "If you care for your world and those in it, you'll be there, along with the fox."

Cuniculus went to strike him with a blast of wind, flying through the air. He dropped out of sight, vanishing into blackness. The ground below her opened up, and she fell, flailing amongst the blackness. Not knowing what was up and down, she cried out with fear. Then, a hand reached for her paw, being the monster female. Her body glowed, lighting up the darkness enough for Cuniculus to feel calmer. "It's you. I know you somehow."

When her finger touched the tip of her claw, Cuniculus felt a sense of peace wash over her. "I will be with you." Smiling at the female, Cuniculus shut her eyes, giving in to the weightless feeling.

She woke suddenly from her sleep, painting with shock and seeing Vulpes slumber soundly. Thinking about the dream, she figured it was just a nightmare and nothing more. For it wasn't uncommon to dream of the monster being tormented still. Even Vulpes jumped up once or twice during the night, his heart pounding and sweat rolling down his brow. With a sigh, she curled up close to Vulpes, settling back down to sleep once more.

By sunrise, Cuniculus left and returned to the warren, welcomed by Diana. The hours flew by. She played with the kittens, spoke with her family, and helped dig more tunnels, making more headway than the rest. After the busy day, she hopped out of the warren and looked up at the sky, seeing Solis set behind the rolling hills in the distance. With a grin, she went to the edge of the forest, eager and ready to see her friend again. She was about to take off running when a voice caught her attention.

"So, going off to see the buck again?" It was Diana, pocking her head out of the warren. "You wouldn't leave without saying goodbye?"

"No, of course not. How could I forget." Turning around and hopping close to Diana, Cuniculus gave a wide smile. "I love you, Mother, and I'll see you when Solis rises over the tree line."

"I'll be here, waiting for you like I always do."

"I look forward to it." Cuniculus nuzzled Diana before she hopped off down the hill and into the brush out of sight. "I love you!"

Diana waited for a few moments, ears folding back with a hint of worry on her face. "Be safe," Diana whispered, praying to Solis to keep her daughter safe on the long and dangerous journey. "Help her return to us, Great Mother." With a sigh, she turned and went back to the others. Some of her grandkids asked her questions, bouncing up and down with happiness. She smiled and went along with the kittens following after her.

* * *

Cuniculus ran as fast as she could, journeying in no time. She rounded a shrub, and what she saw made her do a double take. There was a cluster of greens and a few flowers that sat in a welcoming manner. Besides the pile of green arrangement was Vulpes, looking tall and beaming with glee.

"What in Solis' name is all this for, darling?"

"I hope ya like them. I call it eatin' arrangements or somethin' like that."

"They look beautiful, like the handsome fox next to them." Walking over, she chomped on a leaf, grinning at the taste of the crunchy plant and feeling it break apart in her mouth. With a gulp, she swallowed and moved aside. "Want some, dearie?"

"I ate before ya came. Also, greens aren't my thing. Besides, I didn't think ya'd want to see me eat a fish. The last time ya saw me eat, ya turned away with disguised. I don't want to scare ya away again."

"That was a lifetime ago. Besides, if I recall correctly, Vulpes dear, you pretended it was me you ate upon."

"Ouch, I was hopin' ya wouldn't remember that part."

"It is very different now." She smiled and enjoyed the silence.

They sat for a while, watching Solis set across the horizon. Side by side, Cuniculus leaned her head against Vulpes, whose tail swept back and forth till it lay around her small body. Once it grew dark, they went down the slack run and entered the den. Cuniculus glanced up and, with a surprised expression, saw something that caught her attention. In the middle of the den was a circular bed of rock with flowers in it, making the place smell nice and sweet. The way a field smelled in early spring when the blossoms were in full bloom.

"Going all out, aren't we?"

"It's been a season cycle and over since we've met. I thought it'd be nice to have a softer nest. Ya know, other than layin' on the dirt." He turned and noticed her eyes well with tears. Not expecting such a response, he didn't know what to do. "Sheila, ya, all right? I'm sorry if ya don't like wha' I did."

"It's not you. It's me. This is so very sweet of you, darling. You remember the day we met, cuss, I forgot. You bring the best food for me, build this nest, yet I have nothing for you." She wiped a paw over her face. "I have nothing to offer you."

"I wouldn't say that, ya bein' my friend is more than enough for this fox."

"Yes, but I could've at least caught you a fish or something."

"I didn't do this for ya to return me somethin'. I expect nothin'. I just wanted to give ya good evenin', one worthy of our friendship." He walked over to her, licking her tears away. "I care deeply for ya."

This only broke her heart. "Vulpes, you mean so much to me too." Blinking back her tears, she felt a lump in her throat.

"That's good to hear. Now, wha' is wrong, wha' has you so upset?"

"I, I should've told you this sooner, but I didn't want to ruin what we have. It's so special to me, more than you could imagine. But I can't keep lying to you, darling. I can't hide it any longer."

"I think I know wha' yer going to say-"

Turning, she shook her head and spoke out, cutting him off before he could break her heart. "Don't say it. I know you think I'm weird and that I'm some freak. I know it's unnatural that it might be wrong, but there's no rule saying we can't live together. It seems so unfair, Vulpes."

"Yer right and I want ya to stay with me too. Truth is, I like havin' ya 'round. I don't care if I'm a predator and yer prey. I don't want to go back to the lonely life I once lived." He reached a paw out and ran it along her cheek. "Life without ya would be no fun, be kinda borin'."

"Oh, Vulpes, dear!" She leaped off the ground in a powerful bound, knocking him off his feet. Nuzzling and burrowing into his exposed chest, she wanted to be so close to him. "That's wonderful, what these ears have longed to hear."

He lay on his back and blinked a few times, wondering what just happened, until he felt her paw on him. Placing a paw on her body, he felt her soft fur along his pads. "Cuniculus, I was wonderin' if-if ya would allow me the honor of groomin' ya?"

"G-groom me?" She asked, looking up with a flushed face. "I've never had another mammal groom me before, other than a family member."

Feeling bad for moving too fast, he tried to clarify. "That was too straightforward. I apologize. We only just admitted our true feelings. And here I am openin' my big mouth-"

"I never said no, darling." She spoke, stopping his rambling.

"Then, ya will allow me to groom ya?"

"Yes, I'd adore having you groom me."

He gave her a nod, holding a shy expression as he made the first move. Her heart raced with anticipation, knowing she was about to share a special moment with him. He slowly began to wash her face, then her long ears. Holding her close, he nuzzled his nose into her soft fur. It tickled yet gave him a warm sensation, a pleasant feeling. After he finished washing her, he lay down and she crawled onto him, grooming him back. He purred, and his tail wagged while she brushed his thick fur, taking her time. His muzzle was long, and his nose was wet. She burrowed it. She rested her chin on his nose, gazing deep into his eyes. She could gaze into his eyes forever, hating to even blink.

Tapping her paw playfully to his muzzle, she spoke softly. "So, what now?"

"Well, perhaps someday ya'd let me scent mark ya."

Arching a brow, she wondered what the strange term meant. "Whatever is that? The only mark that comes to mind is when you go out and mark your territory."

"It's not at all like that. Otherwise, I'd never ask such a thing from ya." He adjusted himself, taking a breath before he went on. "Males, like me, have glans in their muzzle, and when we nuzzle, it leaves a scent on the female. It's your choice if ya'd have me as yer mate, that is?"

There was no thinking. She knew the answer. "Yes, I would like to have you as my mate." She cuddled up by his side, and his body curled around her, wrapping her in a ball of red fur. Playing with his tail in her tiny paw, she combed it tenderly. "I don't know how this night could get any better."

"Every night is better when yer here, Sheila." Vulpes smiled and laid his muzzle over her, giving her a gentle lick. "Night."

"Good night, Vulpes."

Warm and cozy, it was easy for the pair to find sleep. For once, after so long, neither had a bad dream. Instead, their dreams were that of a future together, one where they spent their days under Solis' light, sleeping in the den. They even imagined meeting the other's family, Vulpes joining Cuniculus to her warren. It was lovely, the idea of growing old together, sharing life. A bright future that was close to coming true.

CHAPTER XV:

The Two-Legger's Wrath

It was late evening, and Diana went around, making sure everyone was settled in. Among the warren, were burrows, where mated pairs cuddled. Some had a litter among them, the kittens huddled in a sea of fluff. There were many halls, but the large space was where they slept, as it was the warmest. The warren was wide, thanks to the tree roots that held up the ceiling. It was Cuniculus' idea to build it along a tree, getting the layout from her buck friend. How Diana wished to meet him one day, hearing about him through her daughter.

Regardless, Diana made her round, checking, and making sure all was settled before she retreated to her burrow. When she went to lie down, the sound of digging from above stopped her, forcing her to get up and see what was happening. She hoped the warren wasn't caving in, for it happened from time to time. But it wasn't that. It was something strange, digging, unlike any animal she'd heard. All ears and heads shot up, wondering what it could be. Dirt crumbled down, and a slight shake woke some of the kittens.

"Mother, what's going on?" One asked, turning to settle her young down.

"I don't know, but I'll go see." Diana went to the slack run, but before she could leave, the dirt fell in front of her. Trying to move it, more poured down, blocking the run itself. She sat back and felt something was wrong. It wasn't what a normal predator would do.

The group in the warren became quiet when they heard a hissing sound down the hall, along with cries of fright. Out from the dark hall, a buck ran, foaming at the mouth and coughing. He smelled awful and was going out of his mind, ignoring Diana, who tried to talk to him.

"What's wrong with Phil!"

"He looks rabid!"

"Everyone, give him some space." Mother ordered, seeing him claw at any who got too close.

"He doesn't know us"

Phil hissed and went to the slack run, hitting the wall. Suddenly he fell to his side, going into convulsions before he died in a matter of seconds. Diana approached him and saw his eyes were bloodshot, body twitched ever so slightly.

"What could have done this?"

"What's that noise!" Someone cried, looking to where Phill came from.

The fear grew when a cloud rolled in, making everyone cough. Some of the bucks ran to the slack run, trying to move the dirt to escape the bad air or attempt to get it open for their mates and young to escape. Those with a litter stayed and tried to keep the kittens calm while others panicked, seeing the entire slack run was impenetrable. The group trying to leave packed around the run, pushing and shoving to get to the front, digging only an inch or so out. A bit of the gravel was moved, but it became blocked with dead bodies that the living had to cut through. With no fresh air, those still trapped were doomed, and death fell upon them. The sounds of cries for help, squealing kittens, and Diana trying to keep everyone calm filled the warren as no one knew what to do.

✶ ✶ ✶

Above the warren stood the monster. He pulled a spout out of the hole, blocking it with dirt. He waited with a gun and thought the rabbit might be a part of the warren. Had she been, he assumed she'd dig them out, and he'd catch her. After some time, he realized she wasn't a member, rubbing his neck while the sound of leaves rustling in the cool night breeze.

He stood and hit his recorder, holding it to his face. "Late evening, the message must not have gone through, for the animals didn't turn themselves in. I have taken out another warren, and the rabbit was not among them, so I shall look for the fox now." Clicking his gun in place, he left the blocked hole unmoved by the faint sound of squealing.

* * *

The next day, Cuniculus woke up, batting her eyes a couple of times and glancing around to find Vulpes snoring softly. Making small circles in his fur, she watched his tongue hang out of the side of his opened mouth. With a chuckle, she hopped up to his face, rubbing her small nose with his black one. Beyond the slumbering Vulpes, she saw the light coming down the slack run.

"Wake up Vulpes dearie." Cuniculus spoke softly. "Solis is in the sky."

"Can't we just stay and snuggle a little bit longer?" He pulled her close and nuzzled back into the nest. "We had such a wonderful evenin'. Why spoil the mornin' so soon."

"Because I'm hungry." She struggled to try and get out of his grip, being held like a stuffed animal against his chest. Wiggling her body and kicking her legs, it was clear she wasn't going anywhere. "Vulpes, we need to wash."

"Very well, mate." He rolled over and tackled her to the ground, licking her face. "I could just give ya a bath myself."

"I can't share the news with my family if I'm pinned under you, dearie." She sat up and found it hard to believe they were together, after so long, a couple. Her face beamed with joy, matching his expression.

"So, yer gonna do it?" Asked Vulpes in a leery tone, turning back to her. "How are ya gonna explain us?"

"I'll tell them I found a mate, and I'm moving in with him. That he is a fox, a predator who cares for me more than any buck ever could."

"Ya don't have to do this."

"Yes, I do, Vulpes. I'm tired of hiding. It's time to come clean and tell the truth. I'll leave now, and you can come by my warren at high-Solis. I want you to meet my mother. She'll be so happy to see you at long last." Cuniculus felt like a giddy doe in season, unable to contain her joy. "She has been on me to bring you around, so now I can. I can't wait to see the look on her face when she sees you."

"Hopefully, she doesn't die of fear. I'd feel bad killin' her by my mere appearance."

"Don't worry, I'll take care of everything. All you have to do is show up."

"Okay, I'll see ya later, mate."

They headed off in different directions, Cuniculus hopping fast and eager to tell her family the truth. She was in such a hurry that she didn't even stop by the river to bathe. In her mind, she went over what she'd say, hoping Diana was waiting for her by the entrance. When she reached the warren, she looked at the hole. Yet Diana wasn't in her usual spot. No one was there. Not a kit, adult, no one was out grazing. She closed in on the nearest hole and realized the run was covered with dirt. Sniffing the area, the scent of a creature had been there, the grass pressed down by weight. Plus, there was an unusual shape in the dirt.

"Mother!" Cuniculus called in a worried voice, going to one of the other tunnels. "Anyone! Hello, I'm back. Where is everyone? Are you going to jump out and scare me?"

She found all the holes were blocked and grew frightened, thinking back to the nightmare about the monster's threat. If it wasn't a dream and he truly spoke with her, then that meant he was going out of his way to harm others because she nor Vulpes met up with him.

Desperate to reach her family, she dug, digging faster than ever before. Deeper and deeper she went, knowing she was nearing the nesting area. The closer she got, the more determined she was. On the inside of the large area, dirt crumbled, and she tumbled in. There was a haze, and she was unaffected by the poisoned air, the Energy placing a shield around her. She squinted and tried to find her family in the dark, reaching out with her paw.

"Mother? Are you here? If anyone can hear me-" started Cuniculus until she stumbled over something. "Is someone there?"

She realized what she hit was cold, feeling the fur along her paw. It was the outline of a body. Horror filled her, for she knew it was dead, finding corpses all around her. They were her siblings and parents huddled with their kittens. Some of the bodies were torn apart, while most lay on their side. Her chest tightened, her breathing quickened, and she smelled death all around her. She carefully walked through, hoping there might be survivors. Calling aloud, waiting, hoping for a response, yet none followed. Then she found her, Diana. The old doe was in the middle, her siblings huddling around her and lifeless. Tears filled her eyes, streaming down her face.

"N-no!" Cuniculus cried among the dark, throwing herself over the body and mourning. "I'm sorry. Forgive me for not being here!" Backing away, she left the warren of the dead and managed to make her way out, tears running down her face. Not knowing what else to do, she simply lay down and shouted in anger. "Why, why did it have to be them!"

CHAPTER XVI:

The Aftermath

Once Cuniculus left, Vulpes went down the path with a trot in his step. He'd stop by the river, wash, then seek out his sister and brother to tell them the good news. As he walked, he sensed something was off, sniffing the air with a cautious expression. Each step he took sent a ripple out along the earth, allowing him to sense all around him. There were several circles of grey teeth that stuck up and were covered by leaves. He took a step back, knowing whatever it was, was dangerous.

Snap!

The row of teeth clamped shut behind him, causing others to set off. He stomped down, earth keeping them back. When they were all set off, he dropped the rock around him. Quickly, he ran forward, making his way to a hill that overlooked another forest. He painted before smelling smoke and burnt flesh, gazing out to see a horrible sight. The forest was burnt to the ground, and there were several dead bodies. A herd of sheep was caught off guard. He didn't know how the fire spread when there wasn't a storm the night before. With a shake of his head, he went to the river to find his family. Coming to their spot, he heard Reed crying. Something lay before him. Getting closer, he saw it was his sister, only she was dead. The body was stiff and had been there for a while, for the blood on the ground was dry.

"Wha' is goin' on here?"

"V-Vulpes, she's gone." Reed shut his eyes, letting the tears flow.

"How?" Vulpes looked over the body with moist eyes. "There are no bite marks, only a simple dot."

"It was- It was like nothing I've ever seen before. There was a stick that sounded like thunder. Smoke, and before I knew it, she was hit by a black pebble. I tried to help her, but there was nothing I could do." Reed choked and lowered his head, shoulders shaking.

"Who did this? Who would want to kill our sister?"

"Some monster, no doubt."

Vulpes stared down at his sister's lifeless form, angry for being unable to help her. He couldn't wrap his head around it. Why would a creature of the Gods do this? Unless the two-legger wasn't birthed by Solis. It hit him, the realization that the monster wasn't from Animalia but perhaps from another place entirely. That would explain the odd turf, the weird appearance, and the strange abilities. Vulpes knew what needed to be done and had to get to Cuniculus as quickly as possible.

"Listen to me, Reed, ya hide and spread the word to others. Tell them to stay away from anythin' that seems unnatural or dangerous at all cost." Vulpes turned to leave, looking back to Reed, who was confused. "I'll try to be back by high-Luna."

"Vulpes!" Shouted Reed, remaining by the creek. "Where are you going?"

"Somethin' I should've done a while ago." He gave his brother a small smile. "I love ya, brother. Stay safe."

"Vulpes, wait, what do you mean!"

"I'll explain later."

Reed watched Vulpes run into the wood, leaving him behind. Nodding, he did what Vulpes said and spread the word that all should hide till nightfall. Animals, prey, or predators did what was ordered, all aware something dangerous lived among them. All Reed could do was wait and hope for the best that Vulpes would return and let him know what was truly going on. For it was clear there was more to his story than befriending the prey, something changing Vulpes to the core.

Vulpes tracked Cuniculus to her warren; his worst fear was that the monster would find her before he could. When he reached it, he hoped to find her safe with her family. He came out of the brush and went up a small hill and saw her sitting quietly. He rushed to her side.

"Cuniculus, the monster is killin' animals! He killed my sister this mornin'. We need to try and talk to the monster female. She might be the key to stoppin' him."

"Vulpes, I'm so sorry." Said Cuniculus quietly.

"Where are yer family members? Are they underground?"

Tears welled in her eyes, and she broke down, sobbing and clutching him tightly. "It's all my fault. My family, they're dead."

"Oh no." He held her closer, feeling her cling tightly to him. "I'm so sorry. I'm here for ya. I got ya."

"They're gone. And I never got to tell them. I never got to tell mother or say goodbye."

"Let's leave here." He lifted her onto his back and headed to his den.

There they were, Vulpes holding her while she cried. Once she calmed, he fetched her some food and water. For a while, she lay there, full of guilt and grief. He gave her space, not wanting to push her, yet knowing what had to be done.

By noon, he nuzzled her, her eyes still glassy. "Cuniculus, I need to tell ya somethin'. Yer warren, my sister, it was the monster, he killed them. I think he's after us. That he's tryin' to lure us out. I think he wants the items we took."

"I should've been there for them. I should've stopped him or at least died with them." Cuniculus said, getting up and pacing back and forth. "They did not deserve to perish, not in that way, scared, helpless, without a fighting chance."

"No, they didn't. None of them did." Lifting her chin, he met her sorrowful gaze. "He must be stopped from hurtin' anyone else ever again."

"Exactly. I say we give him the items." Cuniculus trembled slightly yet spoke strongly. "Give him what he wants, and he'll leave us be. Leave us to get on with our lives."

"Right, let's go."

They left the den, Vulpes leading the way. The time to reach the monster's dwelling didn't take too long, traveling quickly. Through the woods they went, emerging into the large clearing. There it was, the monster's home, standing tall and menacing as ever.

"So, what's the plan? We storm in and take him by surprise?" Cuniculus looked to Vulpes, who had an expression of uncertainty.

"Maybe, I like yer thinkin'."

They carefully climbed the steps, reaching the front door. Cuniculus glanced from Vulpes to the door, expecting him to open it for them. He rose, standing on his hind legs. Reaching a paw out, moving very slowly to touch the knob. She made a motion with her paw, wanting him to hurry along.

Suddenly he pulled back, pushing Cuniculus forward with his paw. "Why not ya do it, Sheila? After all, with that wind power of ya's, ya can probably knock it right in."

"Such a pup you are." Cuniculus rolled her eyes and took a breath, throwing her paw out to break the door in. The wood flew apart, falling across the floor. "There, was that so hard?"

"Yes, for me, at least."

They entered and were shocked at what they saw, jaws dropping. On each of the walls were heads of animals killed by the monster, mounted with a cold stare. Furs hung over the strange objects in the room, lying across the floor and his nest. It was heartbreaking to see the remains of animals kept as trophies. What was even more horrifying were the stuffed bodies set around the room. At first glance, they looked alive, yet they weren't.

"Gods above, how awful," Cuniculus remarked, looking away. "What do we do now?"

"I'll go out and find him. Cuniculus, perhaps ya should remain-"

"No, if he gets you, then I'll have to save you on top of killing him." Cuniculus lay her paw over his larger one. "We do this together. Remember, I run you chase."

"Ya run I chase. Right, together." Vulpes gave her cheek a quick lick. "Let's go, huntin' mate."

"Never thought I'd see the day when a fox and rabbit went hunting for a two-legger."

They turned from the terrible display, making their way back onto the porch. Before leaving, Vulpes broke the earth around the foundation and let it sink into a pit, setting it ablaze. The fire crackled and danced, smoke rising high into the air. If destroying the monster's home wouldn't get his attention, Vulpes didn't know what could.

"May their souls find peace in the Lands Beyond."

"And rest easy, for Vulpes, and I will keep the living safe."

CHAPTER XVII:

The Gift Is My Heart

Vulpes sniffed the ground, picking up on the monster's scent. He trailed it, followed by Cuniculus, who used the wind and leaped in large bounds. She was behind him till she paused, sensing something was off. Closing her eyes, she felt a dark, cool air go through her body.

Vulpes noticed she fell behind, turning back to her. "Ya okay?"

"Yup, go on. I'll catch up." Giving him a wink, she motioned for him to go on.

"All right." He trotted on, inhaling above the ground.

She lingered back, feeling she was being hunted. When she knew the monster was out there, she spoke. "I know you're here. I sense you."

"Miss me?" A voice asked, looming from behind the brush.

Roughly, she was sent to the ground by a strong force. She moved the drooped ear out of her face and glanced up to find the monster standing before her in his suit. Bravely she spoke. "I'm here to stop your wrath upon this world."

The monster laughed heartily through his mask, stepping closer to her. "Good one. Now you're coming back with me." Throwing his arm out, his Dark Energy surrounded her. He held her still with his left hand and reached down to grab her, chuckling while she trembled to fight against his grip.

"I'll not return with you." Before he could lay a finger on her, she broke free with a blast of wind and cuffed him across the hand.

He drew his hand back, and blood ran through the material, down his wrist, dripping to the ground. "You shouldn't have done that. I was just going easy on you, but now the claws are out!" Electric jumped from his fingers, the monster holding it between his set of hands. He threw the Energy out, sending jolts of lightning at her. She spun through the air, blasting him back with a gust of wind. Skidding on the ground, he struggled to remain on his feet. Cuniculus moved her paw in a circular motion, creating a vortex of wind around him. The cape along his shoulders twisted around his face, spinning round and round. Cuniculus continued her assault. Tangled in his clothes, she went to try and punch him.

With a yell, he glowed again, extending both arms. A red orb of light shot out, throwing the wind back at her.

Paw up, she shielded herself, the wind passing by. When he shot red light at her, she tumbled back, twisting to get on her hind feet once more. Her hacks rose, and her eyes followed his every movement, moving clockwise with him. "Are you going come at me, or are you just going stand there like a fool?"

"My, my, you've changed drastically. Going from a four-legged animal to a more anthropomorphic creature, more civilized than the savage you were."

"The only savage I spot here is you." Cuniculus took step after step, seeing him move opposite from her. "Let's not make a bigger scene. Perhaps we could talk."

"Indeed, for I have much to say. Now that you can communicate with me, having you around makes it more fun."

"I've come to bargain with you. Vulpes and I will give up our powers as long as you leave us and the animals alone."

The monster rubbed a hand to his gas mask, thinking it over. "Very well, you have a deal, rabbit. Now, where is the fox?"

"Right here!" Vulpes came between her and the monster, growling slightly. "Ya, all right, Sheila?"

"She's fine, fox. We've struck up a deal."

"Have ya now?"

"Indeed. Give me the Energy, and I'll let the pair of you be." He held a hand out to them. "You won't ever have to fear the likes of me coming for you again. Now, be a good boy and pass the Energy over."

"Energy? Why can ya just take it from us? Ya had little trouble capturing us."

"Stupid fox, the Energy cannot be taken. It must be given willingly by the host. Otherwise, I'd have seized it long before this."

"Why ya smart mouth, no good son of a b-"

"Okay, enough. Let's pass it to him, Vulpes." Cuniculus stepped forward, placing a paw on his arm. "I wish to get on with our lives, leave this whole thing behind us."

"I guess," Vulpes said with hesitation.

"Wonderful, I'm glad you came to your senses. After all, animals like you could never fully comprehend the power of Energy. Could be quite dangerous in the wrong hands, or, in this case, paws."

Vulpes held a paw up, laying it in front of Cuniculus before she could go to him. "Hold up, Sheila. I have a few more questions for this bloke. Why do ya want this Energy so badly? Ya seem plenty strong to me."

"Sadly, I can't control the elements the way the pair of you can. My powers are limited because of the darkness in them. It taints them, so to speak. Now, please, give it to me."

"Vulpes, quite dawdling." She looked into his eyes, finding only distrust and suspiciousness toward the monster. "I assure you, darling, this is all for the best."

"Yes, believe me-"

Suddenly Vulpes' head snapped up. "Yer lyin', I can feel yer heart racin'."

"What?" Cuniculus turned from him to the monster.

"I may not fully understand ya. But I do know one thing. If he gets more power, he'll be capable of destroyin' three times wha' he can now." Vulpes saw the monster twitch with nervousness, glancing from him to Cuniculus with worry. "I'll not give my Energy up. As long as ya live, the world needs us to protect it from ya."

"Miss Cuniculus, certainly, you'll see reason."

Glancing from Vulpes to the monster, she was torn on what to do. She didn't want to cause more trouble, yet Vulpes' words seemed to ring true. The monster certainly wasn't the good-hearted type, hungry for power and caring nothing for life, given the look of his home. It was a lot, and after the loss of her family, her clear mind was clouded with many emotions and grief.

She shut her eyes, hearing a voice in her mind. It didn't belong to her but was the voice of another, a female, no doubt. "Cuniculus, whatever you do, don't give him your Energy. Heed my words carefully. No matter what he tells you, you must not believe his lies and false promises." In her mind, a figure of light was before her, being the monster female stood. It was the girl from her dream, being connected to the Energy somehow. "Vulpes is right. You're the ones who will watch over your world and protect the innocent that he intends to harm. The watches chose you, recognizing your spirits. For in a past life, the pair of you were my parents, and now I'm with you to guide you toward your destiny." The voice faded, Cuniculus feeling Vulpes take her paw.

Opening her eyes, she felt them well with tears, the girl was gone. If it were true and the voice was that of their daughter from their past life, she was the key to helping defeat the monster. She faced the monster, swallowing a few times. "No, change of plans, dearie. I won't give mine up either."

"You ignorant animals!" Yelled the monster, glowing once more. "Two minds, one pair of watches. You're stronger when you're together. But you lack the skills I have to control the Energy."

In an instant, the pair jumped into action. Water flew, changing to ice, shooting at him. Trying to shield the attack, he was upended and sent through the air. A rock rose where he once stood, propelling him skyward. Able to soar, he rounded back and went to hit Vulpes, only for the wind to blast him sideways. The powerful gust sent him to the earth, rolling over and over till he struck a tree, knocking it down.

"Nice shot, Sheila."

"Obnoxious creatures!" Rising, he saw the pair heading at him, readying himself. "You'll be nothing but stains on the earth when I'm finished with you."

He shot red bolts, trying to hit them. Dirt flew from the impact, raining down on them as they tried to flee. Vulpes cartwheeled in the air, lifting giant chunks of earth. Kicking out, he punched, sending them at the monster. They swooshed through the air, closing the space quickly. The monster dove speedily, seeing the rock pass his goggles. One after another, they came, flying by him. Feet planted firmly, he hit back, trying to keep from being struck by the boulders. The red glow shielded him, the rock breaking and falling to the ground. Vulpes leaped out from over the last one, shooting fire down at him. The flames danced, surrounding the monster, who hunched over, cowering down. Using his other paw, he showered the monster in a brilliant glow, hoping to burn him to a crisp. He moved back, raising his arms to halt his attack. With a confident smile, he stood tall. "Got him!"

"I wouldn't be so sure about that." Cuniculus saw the monster rise, standing unharmed in the sea of fire. Cape waving, he huffed and powered up.

"Take this!" The monster aimed right at Cuniculus, who froze at the oncoming sea of red light.

"Sheila!" Vulpes shouted, running to get to her.

Like lightning, it hit the ground, moving faster and faster toward her. She wasn't fast enough to block it, only able to shut her eyes and throw her arm up. The beam of light never struck, hitting something else. Opening her eyes, she found Vulpes standing in front of her, taking the full brunt of the hit. Given his fire assisted him with speed, he could quickly cross the space and protect her.

The Dark Energy hit, and Vulpes felt jolts of electricity surge through his body, causing his nervous system to break down and his heart unable to take the voltage. His chest was tight, and his heart raced out of control. All he could do was stand there and hope he wouldn't be blown apart, knowing the volts spread to every part of him. When the monster lowered his arms, he laughed and was probably smiling behind his masked face. Vulpes was unable to stand, falling to the ground. He lay there and tried to catch his breath, struggling to fill his lungs. His limbs were unresponsive, numb, luckily.

"Vulpes!" Shouted Cuniculus, rushing to his side. "Vulpes, can you hear me?"

Dropping to her knees, she reached out and held him close, seeing his eyes slowly open. The fur on his body was singed, revealing burnt skin. She smelled the awful scent of it, filling her with anger. The monster took her family, and now, he hurt Vulpes, her mate.

Vulpes in a shaky breath, struggled to speak at first. "C-Cuniculus, ya didn't get hurt. I'm glad." Grinning weakly, he was unable to move.

"Vulpes, let me help you." She tried to think of what to do, hoping to heal him or something. Lifting her paw, water moved to touch his brunt flesh, unable to regrow the fur. "Hold on, just hold on."

His eyes grew moist, and he couldn't shake his head. "There's nothin' ya can do. Besides, I can't even feel my body, so no worries there. I'm not in any pain, Sheila."

Tears welled in her eyes, and helplessness washed over her. "Is there nothing I can do for you?"

"Allow me to scent-mark ya," Vulpes whispered. "I can rest in peace knowin' I belonged to ya."

With a trembling breath, she leaned over and brushed her cheek to his muzzle. Her face moved against his long muzzle, burrowing to feel his warmth. She sniffed and tried not to cry, but the tears ran down her cheek and onto his face. After a few strokes, she planted a small lick on his face.

He moaned, shutting his eyes. "Oh, I wish I could feel yer touch."

Blinking, she gazed down and spoke. "Vulpes, I love you."

"I love ya too, Corinna." Tears ran down his face, calling her by an odd name. "I know we'll meet again after this."

"Corinna?" Before she could say any more, his body went limp in her hold. She shook, unable to believe he was truly gone. Throwing herself over him, she ignored the world around her. She didn't care that the monster was closing in, glowing bright red once more. Nothing mattered for Vulpes was gone. The last of her family, venturing into the Lands Beyond.

The monster raised a hand. "How sad, but you'll join him shortly."

"He was good, and you killed him," Cuniculus muttered under her breath, huddling down over Vulpes.

"You should have given me the Energy. Then he might still be alive." He said, glowing red and preparing to take her down next. "Farewell, rabbit."

CHAPTER XVIII:

Mates for Life

Cuniculus shut her eyes and held tight to Vulpes, accepting her fate. Suddenly, Cuniculus realized it. At that moment, she and Vulpes were reincarnated. Their past names were Corinna and Cornelius, being similar to the monster. A series of images flashed through her mind, a life that they lived before. It was a different world where monstrous two-leggers roamed. Their life together was filled with joy, and they had a daughter, the female monster who spoke to her. The power they had, connected all three of them to the Energy placed in the watches, which bonded them, even after death.

While her eyes were shut, she found herself in a strange place. It was similar to the forest, only it was white, with a light golden glow. Glancing left to right, she saw a shape, a figure appearing before her. It was her, the monster female. Unlike the male monster, she wore jeans, a white tank, and an unbuttoned officer's uniform whipped along her sides. Her eyes were brown, with dark brown hair and tan skin, along with a beauty mark under her left lip, similar to Corinna's dot.

The female stood over Corinna, smiling with recognition. "Hello there, Corinna."

"Hello. W-where are we? Am I dead?"

Shaking her head, she spoke on. "No, you are perfectly fine for now."

They were alone, Corinna looking up at the female. A glow surrounded her, matching Corinna's light. The female's arm extended, and she reached a shaky paw up to hold her hand, feeling a jolt of power pass between them.

"Mom, Dad's Energy is now yours." Said the female, light passing from Cornelius' body to Corinna. "Use it to defeat him."

"But how? He's too strong."

"By using a special ability, he has not mastered and most likely never will. But be leery, for your body won't be able to handle it, and you'll perish afterward. The same fate befell me when he and I battled before." Giving Corinna a sorrowful expression, she continued. "Are you ready for that sacrifice?"

"For the sake of others, yes," Corinna spoke bravely.

"Very well." The monster female placed her hand on Corinna's forehead, transferring her Energy to her. "My name is Cora, and I'll be with you. Both Cornelius and I."

While Corinna was unmoved, the monster raised his hand, taking the chance to power up. Lightening shot out of either hand, sending dirt flying. The image of Corinna was seen along the clear surface of his goggles, flashing white and red.

"Prepare to die!" He was ready to strike when the wind whipped out, sending him backward.

Rolling along the ground, he managed to place his foot down, sliding a few yards back. He collected himself, seeing Corinna illuminated in a sea of golden light. She slowly rose to her feet, drawing water around the ball of air that swirled around her hoovering form. When her face lifted, her eyes glowed solid yellow. For once, since he got there, the monster felt a twinge of fear. For the image of a powered-up Cora flashed, each time the light flicked between the three of them, Corinna, Cornelius, and Cora, the three become one.

"I-it's not possible." He staggered to stand, shoulders shaking slightly. "How are you in the Powerful-State?"

"A woman named Cora helped me see the light."

"This changes nothing. Even if you win, I'll be born again. I made sure of it. We'll see each other in another life and time."

Corinna only smiled. "I look forward to it, dearie." Water shot out, becoming ice and striking him.

When he tried to shield himself, she flew forward, drawing her arm back and sending it forward with a mighty swing. It made its mark, breaking the mask from his mouth. The blow sent him spinning and landing harshly on the ground. He grasped his mouth, blood pouring out. Frantically, he tried to flee, knowing without the face cover, he was at her mercy.

"Not so fast, darling." Arm raised, air shot around his head, stopping him in his tracks. "I know why you feared me most, for I control air. Which was why Cornelius saved me, knowing I'd defeat you. Air gives life, but it can take it away as well."

"You'll die as well!" The monster yelled over the sound of the wind, clutching his neck. He dropped to his knees on shaky limbs, finding it hard to breathe. "I can never be destroyed, not as long as the Energy flows through my body."

"And Cornelius and I will kill you till it's gone." Corinna smiled and yanked the last breath from his body.

The monster dropped to the earth, dead, turning to dust before her eyes. Coming out of the powerful state, she slumped to the ground, unable to move out of pain. Everything on the inside burned, causing her to curl in on herself. Knowing her time was running out, she felt joy that she'd join Cornelius and her family in the Lands Beyond. She'd reunite with her daughter, Cora, and perhaps see others from the past too. Not to mention her siblings and members of the warren. She chuckled and felt tears run down her face, placing a paw on her chest, the beating of her heart slowing down, making taking each breath a struggle.

"I'll be there shortly, Cornelius." whispered Corinna, shutting her eyes. "Cora, I'm sorry I failed. He was too much and will live again."

"Don't worry. You and Cornelius will be there to stop him."

"What about you?"

"I'll be with you both through all of our lifetimes to come." With her words of encouragement, Corinna shut her eyes and gave in. Her body became still, taking one last breath of life. The yellow glow slowly floated out of her, disappearing into the air. Where she collapsed was by Cornelius's body, their paws touching, as though even in death, they wanted to be close.

From afar, Reed saw what happened, how Cornelius and Corinna gave their lives to protect not only him but all animal kind from the monster. While he didn't like prey, he found her bravery to be inspiring, thinking of how he could honor them both. Thus, all he came across he told of a new legend, one where a pair of brave animals fought a monster from another world. A monster who planned on destroying all life and good that Mother Solis and Father Luna created. A story he'd pass on, told from generation after generation, a fable that spread like wildfire. The tale of the fox, the rabbit, and the monster.